בס"ד

More Precious Than Gold

ॐ   ॐ   ॐ

by Evelyn Mizrahi Blatt

with Eve-Lynn J. Gardner

illustrated by Eli Toron

Hachai
PUBLISHING

More Precious Than Gold

First Edition
Av 5762 / August 2002

*To Marty Blatt, whose encouragement was
as constant as his smile. E.M.B.*

Editor: D. L. Rosenfeld
Layout: Yitzchok Turner
Cover Design: Avraham Weg

ISBN: 978-1-929628-10-0

HACHAI PUBLISHING
Brooklyn, New York
Tel 718-633-0100 Fax 718-633-0103
www.hachai.com – info@hachai.com

Table of Contents

Introduction

Unlike other historical fiction of the Spanish Inquisition period, this is not a tale of Jews who chose to remain in Spain and keep their faith in secret, at the risk of their lives. The heroes of this story are the Jews who sacrificed their wealth, their homes and all that was familiar to settle in different lands and openly observe Judaism. This historical, fun to read adventure was carefully researched. All the food items described were taken from authentic recipes commonly eaten in Spain at that time. In keeping with the setting of the story, the spelling of Hebrew words and phrases is consistent with Sephardic pronunciation, and a few Spanish words are sprinkled throughout the text.

Meet the Family

 Sara Mizrahi – This 11-year-old girl, called "Sarita" by her parents, lived a wealthy, comfortable life in Spain.

 Mamá – A gentle, courageous woman, Doña Mazal is determined that her children will live openly as Jews.

 Eva – A simple Spanish woman who has worked for the Mizrahi Family for years, Eva is their last loyal servant.

 Yosef Mizrahi – Sara's little five-year-old brother looks to her for comfort when they leave their familiar life behind.

 **Papá –** Doctor Mizrahi does his best to help the sick and protect his family on their dangerous journey.

 Devorah – This poor orphan was desperate to leave Spain and escape the clutches of the priests.

Spanish Glossary and Pronunciation Key

Bolded syllables are stressed.
The letter "r" is pronounced by rolling the tongue against the palate.

Arroz con garbanzos (a-**ros** con gar-**ban**-zos) – rice with beans

Don – Sir, a title linked with a first name

Doña (**don**-ya) – Lady, a title linked with a first name

Huevos haminados (**we**-vos ami-**na**-dos) – cooked, hard-boiled eggs

Mamá (ma-**ma**) – Mother

Maravedís (mara-ve-**dees**) – a Spanish coin of the period

Mermelada (mer-me-**la**-da) – sweet fruit preserves

Papá (pa-**pa**) – Father

Pescado (pes-**ca**-do) – fish

Señor (sen-**yor**) – Mister, a title linked with a last name

Señora (sen-**yo**-ra) – Mrs., a title linked with a last name

Chapter 1

Changes for Sarita

Cordoba, Spain–1492

 Squinting her dark, almond-shaped eyes against the sunlight that filtered through the shutters, Sara sighed. The trees and flowers looked so beautiful at this time of year! Perhaps her friend Raquel would come over today and they could pick some of the bitter oranges for Mamá to use in her cooking.

Suddenly, a Spanish nobleman on horseback galloped up to the house and stopped just beneath Sara's window.

"Mamá," she called anxiously.

Señora Mazal Mizrahi, a tall slender woman with warm brown eyes, came gracefully into the room. Her elegant dress was floor-length and narrow at the waist. On her head, she wore a short veil that completely covered her hair. Señora Mizrahi smiled at her ten-year-old daughter and called her by the nickname she'd had since she was a baby.

"What is it, my Sarita?"

"Who is that strange man?" Sara asked fearfully.

She was thinking of her parents'

whispered conversations over the past few months when they thought she and her brother Yosef were asleep. Tiptoeing to the top of the staircase, Sara would peer through the rails of the cast iron banister, and catch snatches of words and phrases that floated up from below: "The Inquisition... they issued a decree... we have to leave... getting worse every day." Sometimes, Sara could hear her mother crying.

Sara's mother walked over to the window and looked out. "Well, Sarita, Papá and I told you and Yosef that our house had to be sold. That must be the new owner looking over the property. It has been four months since King Ferdinand and Queen Isabella ordered all Jews to give up our faith or leave Spain. We must leave by the 9th of Av, a sad day indeed," Mamá stroked Sara's dark curls gently with one hand.

"But *why*?" Sara cried. "This has

always been *our* house! Cordoba is our home! Why can't we just pretend to live and pray as the non-Jews do? The King and Queen will never find out. We can be Jewish in secret like my friend Raquel's family!"

Mamá's gentle eyes blazed with strength. "Don't you see Sarita, those who stay and pretend think that nothing will change. They think their children will love Shabbat even if they spend it hidden down in the cellar. They think their children will feel Jewish in their hearts while they pray with priests.

"Your father and I want you and your brother to live openly and proudly as Jews... even if it means we must sell all we have for so little... even if it means we must leave our beautiful home and our lovely garden. Torah and mitzvot, my dear daughter, are more precious than gold."

Sara's cheeks were wet with tears. "I

know all that, but I'm not as brave as you and Papá. I don't want to leave our house and my friends, and..."

"Shh, shh, you are braver than you realize," Mamá murmured, rocking Sara in her arms. "Hashem will always provide for us and protect us, no matter where we live. Now come, dry your eyes," she said, handing Sara a large white handkerchief. "Tonight is Shabbat, and the challah isn't going to bake itself."

Sara wiped her eyes and followed her mother into the large, sunny kitchen. She felt comforted watching Mamá's strong capable hands take a ball of dough from yesterday's bread and dissolve it in a bowl of warm water. Little by little, Mamá poured the mixture into another bowl that held the flour and a small handful of salt. Sara leaned on the long wooden table that stood in the center of the room. She loved to see the way

Mamá mixed all the ingredients into a large mound of dough for challah.

"Mamá, where did you and Papá decide we should go when we leave Spain?"

Mamá sprinkled flour on top of the table and turned out the dough on the smooth surface before she answered.

"We're going to the Ottoman Empire ruled by the Sultan Bayezid." Mamá's hands pushed the dough back and forth to smooth out the lumps. "Do you know what he said just a short time ago? 'If the Spanish rulers are foolish enough to send away their Jews, their loss will be our gain.'"

Mamá brushed off her floury hands and smiled at her daughter. "Papá and I liked the sound of that. Hashem has provided us with a place where we can continue to live as Jews."

"Now Sarita, watch how I knead the dough so that it gets very smooth and silky,"

Mamá said. "That's the secret to making perfect challah. All the women in my family have been making challah this way for generations, and someday, so will you."

"Oh, but can I do it now? Please let me try!" Sara begged. For the moment, she forgot her heartache at the thought of leaving Spain. Mamá smiled as she pulled off a chunk of dough and handed it to Sara.

Gritting her teeth, Sara tried to roll it smoothly along the table, but the dough kept sticking to her fingers. Even after Mamá sprinkled more flour on the table and on her daughter's hands, Sara couldn't seem to get it right. "Don't worry," Mamá said, as she finished kneading Sara's dough. "It just takes practice. It took me a while to learn how to work the dough, too."

Mamá gently placed the dough into the bowl, covered it with a blanket to help it rise, and wiped the flour off her hands. "Will

I ever be able to make challah like you?" Sara asked.

Mamá smiled at her daughter's eager question. "Of course you will, Sarita. I am teaching you just as my mother taught me."

Sara put on her cloak, making sure the bright yellow badge that all Jews had to wear on the right shoulder of their clothing could be clearly seen. Mamá picked up a basket, and the two of them set out to shop for Shabbat.

"Will we have to wear these awful yellow things in our new home?" Sara asked.

Mamá squeezed Sara's hand. "No, Sarita. We are to be welcomed and treated just like everyone else. Hashem has provided a safe place for us to settle while we wait for Mashiach to come."

Together, Mamá and Sara pushed their way through the throngs of people crowding the marketplace. What a busy scene! Chickens clucked and scolded; children begged for a taste of the nuts and fresh fruits on display; oxen and goats plodded along behind their new owners.

As Sara passed by the spice vendor, she closed her eyes for a moment, savoring the strong scents of ginger, pepper and cinnamon that tickled her nose.

"You want *how* much for this tiny vase?" As a customer began arguing with the pottery vendor about his prices, Sara opened her eyes and giggled softly.

"Come Sarita," Mamá broke in, taking Sara by the hand. "Now what do we need?" she murmured.

Sara bounced up and down excitedly. "Aren't we going to make your special fish for our last Shabbat in Spain?" she asked. Nobody prepared *pescado* as delicious as her mother's!

"Absolutely," Mamá said. "If I can just find Yehuda. Where is he today?" she muttered, as they elbowed their way through the crowds, finally stopping in front of Yehuda's baskets full of fat, slippery fish.

Sara stared at the fish, wrinkling her nose at the smell. "Why does fish smell so much better once it's cooked?" she started to ask, when a short dark man suddenly pushed past them, an angry scowl twisting his features. "Spain will be a better place once all you Jews are gone," he snarled over his shoulder.

Sara shrank back with fright, as Mamá wrapped a protective arm around her daughter. "It's all right Sarita; the man's gone now," Mamá said calmly, as the tall, lanky fish vendor turned towards them.

After choosing and paying for a large, fresh fish, Mamá asked, "How have you been Yehuda? My husband didn't see you at the synagogue this week. Is everything all right?" she asked, lowering her voice to a whisper.

Yehuda looked uneasily at the crowds of people swarming around them. "Señora Mizrahi, we, well, I – my name is John now," he said, quickly thrusting the package of fish into her hands.

His name was what? Sara realized that

for Yehuda and his wife, the pretending had already begun. She looked up at her mother, and saw a worried frown flicker across her face. Shaking her head wearily, Mamá turned to go.

Suddenly Yehuda leaned forward and mumbled, "Señora, you and Moshe take care. I heard some men talking in the square this morning. The soldiers are going to enter Jewish homes and take any valuables they find. Give them whatever they ask for, and you and your family should be safe."

Mamá looked sadly at Yehuda. "Thank you for the warning. Please tell your wife I said goodbye," she added softly.

"Mamá, what did he mean?" Sara asked, "What soldiers?" "Shh," Mamá said abruptly, grabbing Sara's hand. "We only have a few more hours until Shabbat starts. Come." As they began walking home, Sara glanced longingly over her shoulder at the familiar marketplace, craning her neck to see the hustle and bustle of the crowds.

What would it be like to shop in a strange new country? Sara felt that everything she did now was full of meaning, and that she had to imprint it all in her memory. This was the last trip to the Cordoba marketplace, perhaps her last walk up this street for the rest of her life. Her mother's voice broke into Sara's thoughts.

"Hurry, Sarita! Why are you walking so slowly? Shabbat is almost here."

In spite of her serious mood, Sara almost laughed out loud. Mamá was in a rush every Friday, and no matter where they went to start a new life, that was sure to stay the same!

Chapter 2
The Challenge

After the heat and noise of the marketplace, Sara was so glad to be home. She and her mother placed their packages on the table in the kitchen.

"Mamá," Sara asked hesitantly, her thoughts still racing about what the fish vendor had said earlier. "What was Yehuda talking about? Why are soldiers coming here? What did we do?"

Mamá sighed, sinking heavily into one of the wooden chairs that stood against the kitchen wall and pulling Sara onto her lap.

"We didn't do anything, Sarita," Mamá said, rocking her daughter comfortingly. "But the king will not let us take any valuable metal out of Spain. The soldiers are coming here to go through our trunks and remove anything they want."

"Will they take my silver bracelets, and my new gold ring that you and Papá gave me for my last birthday?" Sara asked.

"They might," Mamá answered.

Sara's eyes flashed with anger. "But that's not fair!" she cried.

"No it's not," Mamá agreed. "Nothing about this is fair. You didn't realize, but no one would offer us a fair price for our beautiful house. They knew we had no choice but to get rid of it."

Sara was curious. "So how did Papá find a buyer?" She thought about the richly dressed nobleman she had seen that morning.

Mamá had tears in her eyes as she answered. "He couldn't. He traded the house for a donkey and cart to take us to the ship."

Sara was shocked into silence. A whole

house for a donkey and cart! She suddenly felt years older. Perhaps it was her turn to comfort her mother.

"Mamá," she began, "I think the most important things we take with us will be each other and our courage. I can get other bracelets and rings someday."

Señora Mizrahi looked at her daughter with pride.

"I think you are more grown up than I realized, Sara. Come, let's finish making the challah for our last Shabbat in this house."

Just then, a short, round woman with merry brown eyes and rosy cheeks, bustled into the kitchen. Her face broke into a warm smile when she saw Sara and her mother.

"Eva!" Sara cried, flinging her arms around the woman's waist. Eva wasn't Jewish, but she hadn't deserted them like the other servants. Eva had helped Mamá with the house ever since Sara was born and acted like one of the family.

"My Sarita, how are you?" Eva smiled, giving Sara a gentle squeeze, before beginning her cleaning.

"I'm well, thank G-d," Sara replied.

"Eva, good to see you," Mamá said. "Your parents are well, I hope?"

"Very well, Doña Mazal," Eva replied, her voice cracking suddenly. Looking down, the short woman's shoulders began to shake.

Gently, Mamá walked over to Eva and put an arm around her. "Now, now, there's no reason for tears, Eva. Everything will be fine. Perhaps the new owners of our house will keep you on to work for them."

Eva shook her head slowly, and took a deep breath. "I'm not worried about myself at all. I just can't bear the thought of you leaving. You're my second family. It's all so senseless and cruel..."

"It's good to know that not all Spaniards agree with the King and Queen's decree," Mamá said quietly. "We will remember your goodness, Eva, as well as your loyalty."

Then, before tears could come, Mamá turned to Sara and asked briskly, "How does the dough look?"

Sara peered into the wooden bowl where Mamá had placed the smooth, round mountain of dough. It had grown so nicely that it almost reached the top of the bowl. Sara touched the dough gently with one finger and made a small dent, which popped right back out.

"I think it's ready," she announced.

"Wonderful," Mamá said. "Right on schedule. Now, watch!"

Mamá said the bracha and pinched off a small ball of dough. "We take challah, a small bit off of our dough before we bake the rest for ourselves. In the days of the Beit Hamikdash, these pieces of dough were given to the Kohanim who worked in the holy Temple."

Señora Mizrahi stepped over to the hearth and threw the dough straight into the fire to burn.

Mamá took off another chunk of the dough and put it aside. "That is to add to the dough to make it rise next time," she explained.

Deftly, Mamá turned the rest of the dough onto the floured tabletop, and divided it into three parts. She placed one of these in front of Sara and said, "Try to shape it."

Mamá's nimble fingers shaped two perfectly round loaves in no time, while Sara still struggled with her chunk of dough. The more she tried, the harder, flatter, and stickier it became!

"Mamá, it's not working," Sara said, her voice rising with frustration.

"It's all right," Mamá said reassuringly. "It takes time to learn how make challah... and lots of practice." Mamá took Sara's dough and with a gentle touch, formed a round loaf, which she placed on the blanket beside the others. Then she wrapped them all up and left them to rise in the warmth of the kitchen.

"I remember the very first challah that I made all by myself," Mamá said, her eyes turning wistful at the memory. "I was a little older than you are now, and as I put my challah on that special Shabbat plate, your grandmother hugged me and said, "Now the plate is yours," Mamá's lips turned up in a smile at the memory.

"I'd always planned to give you the same chance, Sarita. When you bake a perfect challah all by yourself, that beautiful plate will be my gift to you!"

"Really?" Sara asked excitedly. Then suddenly her face fell as a thought occurred to her. "But it may take years to learn how to make challah by myself, Mamá... what if I never do it right?"

Mamá laughed. "I thought I'd never learn, either. With a little more practice and patience, that plate will be yours sooner than you think!"

As her mother turned her attention to the rest of the cooking, Sara made her way to the large dining room. Afternoon sunlight streamed in through the shutters, and Sara couldn't help thinking that this would be her last Shabbat spent in this special room where her family had celebrated such happy times.

Sara stopped in front of the heavy wooden cabinet that used to hold all her mother's best dishes. They, along with most of the Mizrahi Family's nicest things, had been sold over the past few weeks in preparation for their move. Sara opened the carved doors and carefully took an oval silver plate off one of the shelves.

This plate had graced the Shabbat table in her home for as long as Sara could remember. Now she looked at it as if seeing it for the first time. Gently, she ran her fingertips over the plate's ornate border of flowers and doves. The words *Shabbat Shalom* had been engraved in the center of the lovely pattern, and Sara traced the letters with her finger, imagining the day when she would bake the perfect challah.

She could just picture the proud look on her mother's face and hear her say, "I knew you could do it, Sarita. Now this plate belongs to you!"

"Perhaps I'll have a daughter when I grow up," Sara thought. "A sweet little girl with dark, curly hair. I'll teach her how to bake challah, and when she can do it all by herself, I will give this plate to her!"

"Sarita!" She jumped slightly as the sound of Mamá's voice floated down the hallway, breaking into Sara's daydreams.

"Where did you go? I need you."

"Coming Mamá," Sara called. She hugged the wonderful challah plate and carefully placed it on the table. "You'll see, little plate, I *will* learn to make the perfect challah, and I won't give up before I do!"

Chapter 3

"Soldiers are Coming!"

"Mamá, Mamá, soldiers are coming!" Sara's brother Yosef yelled, as he slammed the front door behind him with a loud bang. "Soldiers are coming!"

"Yosef, are you all right – did any soldiers hurt you?" Mamá, Sara and Eva ran from the kitchen into the main hallway. Yosef shook his head no, and tried to catch his breath.

"Oh Baruch Hashem, you're safe," Mamá said, hugging him tightly.

"I'm fine Mamá," Yosef answered. "I'm not scared. I'm almost six, you know."

In spite of his brave words, the little boy's eyes were wide with fear, and his slender body trembled.

"I was almost on our corner, when suddenly all these soldiers rode past me. I didn't know what was going on, but then three of the soldiers stopped in front of the Diaz's house. They just barged right in." Yosef's face was red with indignation. "They didn't knock or anything!"

Mamá tried to smile reassuringly. "No, I don't suppose they would knock," she said.

"Mamá..." Sara started to say, when suddenly she heard loud, harsh voices and the pounding of horses' hooves from outside.

"The soldiers!" Eva whispered in a frightened voice. "They're coming – they're coming here, right now. Oh, Doña Mazal, what are we going to do?"

Squaring her shoulders, Mamá smiled calmly. "We will wait right here," she answered. "Once the soldiers take all the jewelry and silver that the King and Queen want, they will leave. This will be over soon."

"The soldiers are going to take all the silver?" Sara thought frantically. "But the challah plate – that's silver! The soldiers can't take it! It's going to be my own special treasure someday." Turning, Sara ran down the hall before Mamá could say anything, and grabbed the plate off the dining room table.

Sara looked around frantically for a place to hide the plate. "No, not in the house," she muttered to herself. Desperately, she ran into the garden, holding the plate tightly in both hands.

"Psst, over here – let me have it."

Startled, Sara jumped at the voice coming from the back of the garden. A pale, thin face glanced fearfully through the iron fence. "Did you hear me? Quick, give me the plate – I'll keep it safe for you."

Sara hesitated for a moment, clutching the plate in her arms. Who was this young girl? Could she be trusted? There was no time to be sure. Wildly, Sara thrust the plate into the girl's slender arms, and ran back into the house.

"Sarita, there you are," Mamá said, visibly relieved, as Sara ran over to stand next to her mother. Mamá wrapped a protective arm around Yosef's shoulders.

Boom-boom-boom! They all jumped as the front door suddenly crashed open, and a tall soldier pushed his way inside, the end of his long silver sword slapping against the top of his high black boots.

"We represent their Majesties the King Ferdinand and Queen Isabella," he barked, as four other soldiers streamed in after him, and began pulling tapestries and paintings off the walls. "We are here to see that you Jews do not take any wealth that belongs to the Crown of Spain," he added, looking around the hallway, and adjusting the silver helmet that covered most of his dark black hair.

Mamá nodded her head, and lifted her chin defiantly as the soldier pushed past her. "Where do you keep your jewelry?" he demanded, contempt flashing in his eyes.

"This way," Mamá moved toward the stairs.

"I'll go first," the soldier sneered. "I wouldn't want you Jews to try hiding anything, now would I?"

Anger blazed in Mamá's gentle eyes, as she, Sara and Yosef walked upstairs, behind the rude soldier. The screeching of furniture and the clattering of silverware could be heard coming from the dining room.

"Here is all my jewelry," Mamá said icily, handing the soldier her carved wooden jewelry box.

Opening the lid, the soldier peered inside, smiling as he pulled out a handful of heavy golden chains, a beautiful strand of pearls, and other pieces that had been in the Mizrahi Family for many years.

"What about her," he motioned towards Sara, who moved closer to her mother's side. "What's she got?"

Mamá wrapped a protective arm around Sara's shoulder. "My daughter only has a few things – some bracelets and a little ring – small trinkets that are of no great value to anyone."

"I'll be the judge of that," the soldier barked. "Get them now."

Calmly, Mamá walked across the hall and opened the door to Sara's room. "Here," she said returning a few moments later, putting Sara's silver bracelets and new gold ring down on the bed.

"Not worth anything – nice try," the soldier glared at Sara, scooped up her jewelry and thrust it into the wooden box.

Sara choked back tears of sadness and anger. She would not let this awful soldier see her cry! She dug her fingernails into her hand and repeated her mother's words in her head, over and over. "Torah and mitzvot are more precious than gold. We have something more precious than gold!"

The soldier really seemed to be enjoying himself. He poked through the two trunks that stood in Mamá's room and removed a piece of expensive silk material. "Not much else up here I see," he said. The soldier walked across the hall, and rummaged through the trunks in the other rooms. "All right, that's it," he said a few minutes later.

Sara felt cold sweat trickling down her

back as the soldier clumped his way down the stairs. She glanced at her mother wonderingly. *How could Mamá stay so calm?*

"Well?" the tall soldier asked as the other soldiers poured back into the main hall. One carried a few paintings and tapestries; another lugged a large sack full of silver and other valuables. "Did you get everything?"

"Oh, we got everything all right," a short, stocky soldier answered gleefully, holding up a beautiful Kiddush cup in one hand, and a gold and silver menorah in the other. "These Jews have a lot of nice things."

The tall soldier nodded approvingly and looked over his shoulder at Sara and her family. "A speedy trip to you," he sneered, as the other soldiers marched right out the front door.

"And there is no need to thank us for making your packing so much easier, and your trunks so much lighter." With a nasty laugh, he ripped the silver mezuzah case off the doorframe and was gone.

Everyone stood frozen in place, everyone except Sara. She caught the parchment of the mezuzah just before it hit the ground. Lovingly holding it next to her heart she said, "Look, Mamá! We still have the most precious part to take with us to our new home!"

"You are right, my child," Mamá answered softly.

As the sound of pounding hooves faded away, Mamá hugged Sara and Yosef, then sank into a chair. "Thank G-d they didn't hurt us," she murmured, closing her eyes. Her lips moved in a silent prayer of thankfulness to Hashem that He had protected them all from harm.

Eva appeared in the doorway of the kitchen, wringing her hands in dismay. "Doña Mazal, they took everything,

everything," she moaned.

"I want Papá," Yosef said, his voice cracking.

Mamá opened her eyes, and tried to smile. "All that matters is that we are all safe," she said. Those that stay in Spain will always live in fear of searches like these."

"But Mamá, why would the soldiers keep searching for valuables?" Sara asked, puzzled. "Didn't they take everything already?"

Mamá shook her head. "Those that stay will live in constant fear of searches that prove they are still living secretly as Jews," she answered. "And those searches will never stop. Papá and I refuse to hide. We will live openly as Jews."

"You and Papá are right," Sara said. "And Yosef and I will never hide who we are from the world either. Will we Yosef?" she asked her little brother.

"Never," Yosef agreed.

"But I still wish we didn't have to leave," Sara sighed.

"I know Sarita," Mamá said. "But right now we need to get back to our Shabbat preparations," she added, standing suddenly and walking towards the kitchen. "We've had enough of this kind of excitement. Eva, please lay out Yosef's best Sabbath clothes while I finish the baking."

"Yes, Doña Mazal," Eva replied. She smiled at Yosef and they walked up the stairs together.

Sara followed her mother back into the kitchen. After all this time wrapped up in the warm blanket, the challah loaves had grown until they were almost double in size. She and Mamá took them outside to the clay oven, in which twigs and vines from the garden were burning.

Mamá had always been so happy to have a private oven for baking. It stood outside the house so as not to cause a fire. Families too poor to have their own oven shared with other families or bought bread from the local bakeries.

"I wonder if we'll have our own oven when we move," Sara said.

"Probably not," Mamá answered. "But we can share one like so many others do. The challah will still taste just as good."

When the loaves were half-baked, Sara's mother brushed the top of each one with some water and returned them to the warm surface of the oven. Before long, the bread smelled delicious and had turned a crusty, golden brown.

Sara watched everything more closely than ever before. "If I am to bake the perfect challah," she thought, "I must really pay attention!"

She and her mother took the challah inside to cool.

"Now Sarita, please set the table for Shabbat," Mamá said. "Then go wash up and change your clothes."

"Yes Mamá," Sara replied, walking down the hall and into the dining room. She looked at the walls, stripped of their tapestries, and tears welled up in her eyes. The doors of the carved wooden cabinet stood open, revealing only empty shelves. Sara stood silently for a moment, before remembering the one thing that she missed the most.

"Our challah plate," she whispered. "I gave it to that girl – oh, where is she?"

Sara glanced at the garden fence. No one was there. All of their family treasures were gone forever. Was the lovely silver challah plate gone, too?

Chapter 4

The Orphan

"Sarita, come on!" Sara jumped slightly as Yosef poked his head around the door of her room.

"I'm coming, I'm coming," Sara replied, as she quickly finished brushing her dark curly hair. She held out the pleats of her blue velvet dress, admiring the tiny stitching of gold braid that her mother had sewn around the edges of the sleeves and hem.

Yosef rolled his eyes. "You look fine. We're going to be late if we don't get downstairs," he said impatiently, as Sara took one last look in the mirror. Turning around, Sara smiled at her little brother.

"Come on, I'll race you," she said, running past Yosef, and dashing down the hallway. "All right," Yosef exclaimed delightedly, charging after her. Giggling, Sara and Yosef ran to the top of the stairs before stopping suddenly as Papá's voice floated up to them.

"The soldiers were here? Is everyone all right?" Yosef looked at Sara, who put a finger to her lips, motioning her brother to be quiet. Looking through the slits in the banister, Sara saw Mamá nod her head yes.

"We're all right, Baruch Hashem," Mamá said. "I expected them to take the silver and the jewelry, but they took our menorah and even our mezuzah cover. "Mamá's voice trembled as she said those words.

"At least you and the children weren't harmed," Papá answered, clenching his hands and shaking his head. "I'm so sorry that I wasn't here. I can't bear the thought that you had to face them alone."

Wiping her eyes, Mamá looked up into her husband's warm brown ones and took a deep breath. "I wasn't alone, Moshe," she said quietly. "I had Eva and the children with me, and I knew Hashem wouldn't let any harm come to us."

"Sarita," Yosef tugged on the edge of Sara's sleeve. "Now can we go down?" he hissed loudly. "Shhhh," Sara whispered back, but it was too late. Looking up, Papá and Mamá's faces broke into warm smiles when they saw Sara and Yosef standing at the top of the stairs. "Papá, you're home!" Sara and Yosef called as they raced down the stairs and hurled themselves into his arms.

Kissing the top of his children's heads, Papá closed his eyes and murmured a prayer of thankfulness to Hashem that his family was safe. "Papá, why are you home so late?" Sara asked.

"The new court physician wanted to go over some things, and it took longer than we expected," he said. "But I still have enough time to change and get ready before Shabbat." With that, Papá went upstairs, Yosef trailing behind him.

"Come, Sarita," Mamá said. "Let's

make sure that everything is ready for tonight."

Following her mother into the kitchen, Sara inhaled deeply. "Mmm," she said aloud, savoring the wonderful aroma of chicken, fish, and fresh challah that filled the room. "Everything smells delicious."

"It certainly does," agreed Eva. "Your mother is the best cook, Sarita, and don't you forget it. Doña Mazal," Eva said, putting a bowl of sweet *mermelada* on one of the tables. "Everything is finished. I must go now."

Mamá wrapped her arms around Eva. "Thank you for all that have done for us," she said softly. "We will always remember you with warmth and affection."

Eva nodded, and tried to smile. "Good-bye my Sarita," she said, walking over to where Sara stood. "You remember to mind your Mamá and Papá, and take good care of little Yosef."

"I will. Good-bye, Eva," Sara answered, struggling not to cry as they hugged for the last time.

Walking into the hallway, Mamá pressed several gold *maravedís* into Eva's hand. "Oh no, Doña Mazal," the kind woman protested. "This is too much."

Mamá shook her head. "Nonsense," she said, trying to blink back the tears that started to form in her eyes. "Doctor Mizrahi brought these home especially for you. Good-bye, Eva."

"Good-bye," Eva's voice broke. "May G-d watch over you on your journey, and in your new home."

With tears streaming down her face, Eva turned and ran down the front walk.

"Oh, Mamá," Sara cried, as her mother closed the door. "So many goodbyes." Sara wrapped her arms around her mother's waist.

"Shh, shh," Mamá said, as Sara began to sob quietly. "I know, my child," she murmured, holding her daughter in her arms comfortingly.

After a few minutes, Sara took a deep breath and wiped her eyes and nose on the handkerchief that Mamá handed her. "Better?" Mamá asked.

Sara nodded. "Better," she replied.

"Then come," Mamá said. "It is time."

Papá and Yosef had already left, so the house was very still as Sara and her mother lit the Shabbat flames and said the bracha together.

Sara watched the shadows flickering on the walls. "How can this be our last Shabbat in this house?" she thought despairingly, struggling to swallow the lump that was forming in her throat.

Uncovering her eyes, Mamá's gentle

face glowed in the soft light of the flickering flames. "Shabbat Shalom," she said. "Shabbat will bring us peace."

* * *

Lifting a glass filled to the brim with sweet red wine, Papá smiled at his family as they stood silently around the table later that evening. "Although this isn't my usual Kiddush cup," he said, "though the silver challah plate is gone, and our table isn't set the way it usually is, all that matters is that we are all safe and together to celebrate Shabbat."

"Before Kiddush, Papá," Sara said, " I have to tell you and Mamá about the challah plate. You see..."

Just then came a knock on the back door. Everyone froze, listening as the knocking became louder. "Moshe," Mamá said in a low voice that shook slightly. "Who could that be?"

Calmly, Papá stood and walked towards the door. "I'm sure it's just one of the neighbors, Mazal," he said, opening the door, and peering outside.

Sara gasped. "What are you doing here?" she exclaimed, jumping up, and knocking over her chair in the process. There, standing in the doorway stood the mysterious girl from the garden!

"Sarita, do you know this girl?" Papá asked, staring at the thin, pale child who stood shyly before him.

Running over to the door, Sara smiled, and motioned the girl to come inside. "No, not exactly, Papá," she said, closing the door.

"Then – what, who," Papá raised his eyebrows in surprise.

"Am I too late?" the girl asked Sara in a soft, timid voice.

"Too late for what?" Mamá asked,

walking over to stand next to Papá.

The girl smiled timidly. "I hid this in an old tree stump in your backyard after I saw the soldiers leave the neighborhood this afternoon," she explained, "and I covered it with leaves so no one would find it, but am I too late? Have you already made Kiddush and Ha'motzi?"

Then from under her shabby brown cloak, the girl pulled out the silver challah plate and held it up for everyone to see.

"What in the world!" Mamá exclaimed, taking the plate in her hands, and staring at it in amazement. "I thought the soldiers had taken this with all our other valuables. How is it that you have it?"

The girl twisted her hands together, and looked down at her feet.

"I gave it to her Mamá," Sara declared.

Mamá and Papá looked at Sara in amazement. "When?" Mamá asked.

"I was trying to tell you. It was right before the soldiers came this afternoon," Sara explained. "I couldn't bear the thought of the wicked Ferdinand and Isabella taking our precious challah plate, and when I ran outside to try and hide it, she," Sara pointed to the girl standing beside her, "offered to help me hide it from them."

56

Papá and Mamá smiled. "That was very brave of you both," Papá said. "Yes it was," Mamá agreed. "But please tell us who you are. What is your name?" she asked, putting her arm around the girl.

Shyly, the girl shuffled her feet. "I, I'm Devorah. I'm an orphan, and I live with a Jewish family nearby," she said. "I help them with the cooking and cleaning in return for my room and board.

"I, I know about the Inquisition, and the King and Queen's decree, but the family I live with refuses to leave. They've decided to stay, and pretend they are no longer Jewish. I remember the beautiful Shabbat meals I used to spend with my parents," Devorah's dark eyes suddenly filled with tears.

"I can't bear the thought of not living as a Jew any longer, and I've been praying to Hashem to help me find a way to escape

Spain. Then I saw you and your daughter at the market today and I overheard your conversation with the fish vendor."

Papá looked questioningly at Mamá. "I'll explain later," Mamá said. "Please go on, Devorah," she urged.

"Well," Devorah continued. "When I realized that you were leaving Spain rather than giving up Jewish life, I knew that Hashem had answered my prayers. So I followed you home. I was trying to get up the courage to knock on your door and ask if you could help me, when I heard the soldiers coming, and then she," Devorah pointed to Sara, "ran into the garden holding the plate, and well, you know the rest," she finished.

Mamá slowly rose to her feet, as she and Papá absorbed Devorah's words.

Papá asked Devorah suddenly, "Was your father's name Don Isaac?"

"Why, yes," she answered.

"He was a friend of mine years ago, but we lost touch. I never knew he had a daughter; you look just like him."

"Have you eaten?" Mamá asked softly.

Devorah shook her head no.

"Well, you must eat with us, then," Papá declared. "Please, sit down," he said, walking over to the table and pulling out a chair.

"Thank you," Devorah said timidly.

Yosef grinned at Devorah, "Our Mamá makes the best *arroz con garbanzos* in all of Cordoba," he boasted happily. "And I'm going to eat until I burst!"

Everyone laughed, including Devorah. "Then so am I!" the girl declared.

* * *

"The meal was delicious, Señora Mizrahi," Devorah said later that evening, after Mamá set a plate of fruit on the table. "And thank you, Señor Mizrahi, for your kindness," she added.

Papá's face beamed in the candlelight. "It was our pleasure to have such a special guest for our last Shabbat in Spain," he said.

"When do you have to report to the ship?" Devorah asked quietly.

Papá's face turned somber. "As soon as Shabbat is over, we will load our trunks into the cart. We leave for the port city of Cadiz the next morning."

"Señor," Devora hesitated suddenly, looking down at her hands.

"Yes, Devorah," Papá said.

"I, well, I wanted to know... could I come with you when you leave Spain?" she asked. "Oh please, Señor, Señora! I wouldn't be any trouble, honestly," she declared, the words tumbling out of her mouth so fast it was hard to understand them. "I would work for you and help you – but, please take me with you!"

Papá looked at Mamá, his eyes full of compassion for this young girl. "Devorah, we will do all we can to help you. Let me find out whose permission I need to take you with us. Then everything can be done properly."

Devorah's eyes filled with tears. "I understand, Señor," she said softly. "I wouldn't want to get you into trouble."

"My husband knows a lot of people," Mamá put in. "Perhaps this won't be as difficult as you think."

Devorah nodded. "Thank you," she whispered. Looking outside, she stood suddenly. "I must go now. If they discover that I am here..." she shook her head, as she walked over to the back door and pulled on her cloak.

"Will you be all right walking back by yourself?" Papá asked, a worried frown on his face.

Devorah nodded. "I'll be careful," she

said. "I know which streets the soldiers do not patrol. It wouldn't be safe for any of you to be caught out at this time of night. Thank you again for the meal and for trying to help me. Shabbat Shalom."

And with those words, Devorah waved goodbye, and disappeared into the darkness of the night.

Papá and Mamá looked sadly at each other for a moment. "Come Yosef," Papá said, standing up. "Let us learn together until it's time for bed."

Sara watched her father and brother walk down the dark hallway and into the living room that Eva had lit with lamps before Shabbat. "Mamá," she asked, "Will we be able to help Devorah?"

Mamá sighed, "I hope so, Sarita," she said softly. "Just remember that everything is in Hashem's hands."

Chapter 5
Sara in Charge

"Shavua Tov," Papá said, as he poured the wine over the Havdallah flame, its sizzling hiss signaling the end of Shabbat for that week.

"Shavua Tov," Mamá and the children responded, watching as the thin curl of black smoke spiraled into the air and disappeared.

Sara stared moodily out the window. This was their last night in Cordoba. Tomorrow they would load their cart, travel to the Bay of Cadiz, and board the ship that would take them far away from everything and everyone they knew. Unhappily, Sara walked out of the dining room and down the hall.

"Sarita, come on, let's play a game," Yosef called, skipping past her, and running up the stairs two at a time.

"Not now, Yosef, maybe later," Sara answered, slowly climbing the stairs and walking into her room.

"Later will be bedtime," Yosef whined. But Sara shook her head no, closing the door over her brother's protests.

By the light of the oil lamp that stood on the tall dresser by the door, Sara looked around her room. In one corner sat the chest that had belonged to her great-grandmother. Directly across from it was the cradle in which Mamá had rocked both her and Yosef to sleep when they were little.

Gently lifting the lid of the chest, Sara took out the maroon colored gown that she and Mamá were hemming. Rubbing the soft silk against her cheek, Sara began to twirl around the room, imagining how grown up she would look when this beautiful gown would fit her. Sara twirled and danced until she fell breathlessly onto her bed. Opening her eyes, she watched the leaves blowing on the trees just outside her window.

"I've looked out this window every night before saying my bedtime *Shema* for as long as I can remember," she thought sadly. "But tonight is the last night I'll ever..." Dropping her head in her hands, Sara suddenly began to sob, her tears leaving dark droplets on the gown.

"I guess I'll never get to wear this gown," she whispered a few minutes later, lifting her head and wiping her eyes on the edge of her sleeve. "I can't take any of my best gowns or this cradle, or, anything!" Twisting herself out of the chair, Sara tossed the gown back into the chest, and slammed the lid shut, before throwing herself across her bed, sobbing brokenheartedly.

Hearing her mother's light footsteps in the hall a few minutes later, Sara sat up suddenly, and wiped her eyes with the back of her hand. "Sarita," Mamá called, knocking on the door.

"Yes Mamá, come in," Sara answered, standing up and trying to smooth the wrinkles out of her dress.

"Papá and I have decided to try making Devorah a part of our family," Mamá said. "It's the only way we can take her with us. We are going to speak to one of Papá's patients who is a nobleman of the court. Perhaps he will help arrange this without too much trouble."

A worried frown crossed Mamá's face when she saw Sara's red swollen eyes. "Sarita, is everything all right? You look as though you've been crying," Mamá hurried over to her daughter, and put a hand on Sara's cheek.

Sara nodded, and looked down at her feet. 'I'm all right Mamá," she said bravely. Her problems seemed so small when compared to Devorah's.

Mamá hugged Sara, and kissed the top of her head. "I imagine you're feeling sad about leaving," she said. "Just remember that what we're taking with us..."

"... is more precious than gold. Right, Mamá?" Sara hugged her mother back.

"Exactly," Mamá replied. " Now Papá and I will return as soon as we can. Will you keep an eye on Yosef until we get back?" she asked.

Sara nodded. "Yes, Mamá."

Mamá smiled. "Good. And Sara, Papá and I don't want you to let anyone in the house for any reason... not one of your friends or one of the neighbors... no one, all right?"

Sara nodded again. "I won't let

anyone in the house," she said.

"Good," Blowing her daughter a kiss, Mamá softly closed the door and went looking for her son.

"Yosef, we're leaving for a little while. Do what Sara tells you, and go to bed on time... all right?"

"Yes Mamá," Yosef answered, running down the hall and knocking on Sara's door.

Sara smiled to herself. "Yes, Yosef. You can come in," she said.

"I'm hungry," the little boy told her. Sara sighed.

"Well, would you like to eat some challah before bed?" she asked.

"Okay," shouted Yosef.

Sara ran downstairs for the challah and a knife. Usually they couldn't eat upstairs, but for their last night in Cordoba, Sara was sure her parents wouldn't mind.

After she and Yosef washed their hands, Sara placed a cloth over her dresser and cut a fat slice of leftover challah for both of them. They said the bracha and ate in silence, thinking their own thoughts. Sara helped her brother sing the Birchat Hamazon, and then announced,

"Time for bed!"

"Can we play a game now?" Yosef asked, trying to look sweet. "Please?"

"He is so little," Sara thought. "He doesn't even realize how much our lives will change... how everything has already changed."

She walked over to her brother and gently tweaked the end of his nose. "Okay, but only one game, Yosef. It's late."

The little boy jumped up and ran over to a large box filled with beautifully carved wooden letters. "I want to play the aleph-bet game," he said.

"All right." As Sara dumped the contents of the box onto the floor, Yosef picked up one of the letters. "I'm going to be the gimmel," he declared.

Sara grinned, her hands busily arranging the other letters in a circle. "Then I'm going to be the vav," she exclaimed in a squeaky voice that made Yosef giggle.

Looking around the room, Yosef

stared at the trunk that stood in the corner.

"Sarita," he said.

"Hmmm," Sara replied.

"Why can't we take all our toys with us when we leave Spain?" Yosef asked.

Sara looked into her brother's wide brown eyes, and tried to smile reassuringly.

"Because there's not a lot of room on the ship," she explained. "So we can't take all our things. But don't worry Yosef," she added, forcing herself to sound cheerful. "Once we get settled in our new home, I am sure we will get more toys. Perhaps they'll be even better than the toys we have now!"

"Really?" Yosef asked, his eyes lighting up at the prospect of new and better toys.

Sara smiled, as she leaned over and kissed her little brother's cheek.

"Really," she said.

* * *

"Good night," Sara called softly over her shoulder. She carefully carried a lit lamp in one hand, and closed the door to Yosef's room with the other. Walking quietly down the stairs, Sara made sure that the lamps were still burning in the hallway before passing through the dark kitchen and into the dining room.

Setting the lamp down in the middle of the table, Sara shivered slightly, watching the shadows flickering on the walls and the ceiling. She went over to the carved cabinet to get the silver challah plate.

"I'm going to pack it with my very own things. It will be mine one day, I hope."

Sara mounted the stairs and gently tucked the plate into her trunk beneath some of her clothing. Would the precious silver plate still be there at their journey's end?

Suddenly, Sara heard a little thumping noise coming from the back of the house.

She crept down the stairs, listening intently.

"I wish Mamá and Papá would come home," she whispered uneasily. Even Yosef's company was better than being downstairs all by herself. Suddenly, Sara heard that sound again. Turning around, she jumped. There was a face staring at her through one of the windows!

Sara yelped in fear and backed away.

"Sara, it's Devorah," Sara heard a soft voice call through the window. "I'm sorry; I didn't mean to frighten you."

"Devorah?" Sara said confusedly, running over to the window. "What are you doing here?"

Looking fearfully over her shoulder, Devorah motioned towards the locked back door. "Please, let me in," she implored. "I overheard the woman I live with talking to one of the priests tonight. They told him they suspect I still want to live as a Jew, and will try to run away.

"The priest is planning to send me to an orphanage tonight! I managed to slip away when they thought I was cleaning up the kitchen, but it's only a matter of time before they discover that I am missing. Please help me!"

"But, I, I'm not supposed to let anyone in..." Sara started to say, watching as tears rolled down Devorah's thin, pale face. "What should I do?" she wondered helplessly. "What would Mamá and Papá want me to do?"

Suddenly the sound of hooves pounding down the street reached her ears, and harsh guttural voices barked orders. "Search the gardens and the houses! We need to find that girl tonight!"

Wildly, Sara yanked open the door, and pulled Devorah inside. "Hurry," Sara whispered, closing the door and locking it.

"We've got to hide you right now, or they'll find you."

"Yes, yes," Devorah agreed, as Sara grabbed the girl's hand, and began running towards the stairs. "But where?" she asked, as they raced up the dark staircase and down the hallway.

"I don't know maybe, maybe under the bed?" Sara suggested, opening the door to her room, and pushing Devorah inside. "No, wait, not there," Sara muttered, suddenly pulling Devorah back towards her. "Under the bed is probably one of the first places they'll look."

"Then where can I hide?" Devorah asked.

Sara looked around her room frantically, as the sound of men's voices grew louder and louder!

Suddenly, her eyes fell on the trunk that stood silently in the corner. "There!

We'll hide you in there!" she declared, racing over and lifting the lid.

"But, there's no room," Devorah said, looking inside the fully packed trunk.

"Oh, yes there is," Sara exclaimed, reaching in, and pulling out handful after handful of clothing, and throwing it on top of her bed.

"Oh, Sara, your clothes," Devorah started to protest, but Sara shushed her with a wave of her hand.

Devorah's eyes grew wide with fear as she thought of something else. "Do you know how much trouble hiding me could cause for you and your family, Sara? Are you sure about this?"

"Get in," Sara said helping Devorah step into the trunk, and covering the girl with the few dresses that still remained at the bottom. "You would do the same for me. I know you would. Don't move or make a sound until they leave."

"I won't," Devorah said, her voice muffled under the layers of clothing. "And Sara," she whispered.

"Yes," Sara replied, trying to tuck the clothing more securely on top of Devorah.

"Thank you," Devorah poked a finger up along the side of the trunk.

Taking a deep breath, Sara shook the

finger. "You're welcome," she said. "Now, remember, not a sound."

Racing back downstairs, Sara tried to quell the fear that was rising up inside her like a tidal wave. "Hashem will watch over us," she whispered aloud. "Mamá and Papá will be back any minute, and this will all be over soon."

Boom-boom-boom! Sara jumped as the front door suddenly crashed open, and two priests dressed in long black robes stood in the doorway, flanked on either side by an armed soldier.

"Good evening," the tall priest said, as the shorter one walked over to the kitchen entrance and poked his head inside. "We don't wish to disturb you, but we are searching for a missing girl. She is an orphan, and we need to find her and bring her back to the family she ran away from. She's about your height, with long thin brown hair. Have you seen her tonight?"

What an odd feeling. Sara had never fooled a grown up before. Now Devorah's life and future depended on how well she could fool these men.

Looking the priest straight in the eye, Sara tried to seem confused. "A missing girl? Here? No, I'm sorry. No one's been here tonight."

"Well, I'm sure you won't mind if we take a quick look around," the tall priest said, as the soldiers walked down the hall and began searching the living room and dining room.

Now Sara tried to look scared, which wasn't very hard to do.

"My parents said not to let anyone in... I don't want to get into trouble. Can't you wait until they get back?" her voice was trembling.

"No, we certainly cannot," the shorter

priest replied, walking back into the hallway. "And we're sure your parents would want you to cooperate with us, my child. Now, where are the bedrooms?"

Sara took a deep breath. "This way," she said walking up the stairs, the two priests following behind her.

Sara watched as the priests quickly searched her parents' room. She gasped as the first thing both priests did was to get down on all fours and poke under the bed!

"Is something wrong, my child?" the tall one asked, watching Sara suspiciously.

"No, nothing," Sara replied.

"Sarita?" Sara ran down the hall as Yosef called sleepily for her from his room. "Sarita, I heard a noise!"

Quickly opening Yosef's door, Sara lit the lamp that stood on the dresser, throwing the dim room into brightness.

"Everything is all right, Yosef. Go

back to sleep; these men are just looking for something they lost," she said soothingly, sitting next to Yosef on the bed.

Yosef's eyes grew round with fright as the two priests walked into his bedroom.

"They'll be leaving in a few minutes; everything is all right," she repeated, rubbing Yosef's back as he clung to her. They watched the tall priest throw open the lid of the little boy's trunk and toss everything onto the floor, while the shorter one searched the terrace outside and checked under the bed.

"And where is your room, my child?" the tall priest asked, standing up, and kicking the pile of clothes out of his way.

Sara could feel her heart beating fast; her tongue felt thick and dry with fear. What chance did Devorah have if the priests were emptying the trunks?

Disentangling herself from Yosef's

grip, Sara stood and walked over to the door. "I'll be right back, Yosef," she assured her brother. "You stay here."

Stepping across the hall, Sara opened the door to her room, and stood aside as the priests pushed their way in.

Forcing herself to act calm, Sara watched as they searched her room. Staring at the open lid of Sara's half-filled trunk, the tall priest leaned down and began to reach inside. Holding her breath, Sara watched as his hand drew closer and closer, when...

"Ho, Father," Sara heard one of the soldiers calling from downstairs.

The tall priest quickly walked into the hallway and grabbed the lamp off the table, the other one trailing after him.

"Yes, what is it?" he called impatiently, as Sara let out a sigh of relief.

"We just got a report that the girl was seen north of here a few minutes ago... thought you might want to know," the soldier said.

Nodding, the two priests began walking down the stairs.

"Good, she can't have gone far then," the shorter one declared.

Softly closing her bedroom door, Sara walked down the dark hall, and stood on the landing, watching as the soldiers gathered back into the foyer.

"Find anything?" the tall priest asked. The soldiers shook their heads no.

"All right, let's keep on searching," the shorter one said.

Opening the front door, the tall priest looked up at Sara.

"Thank you for your help, my child," he said smoothly.

"Yes, thank you," the shorter one repeated. "And be sure to have a pleasant trip tomorrow," he added.

Trembling, Sara felt her knees suddenly give way, as she sank to the floor and leaned her head against the staircase railing.

"Boruch Hashem that's over, and Devorah is safe," she whispered. "What a miracle!"

"Sarita!" Lifting her head, Sara heard Yosef calling for her.

"Everything's fine, Yosef," she called, "Go back to sleep."

Sara stood up and took a few deep breaths, trying to quiet the shaky feeling in her chest. Had she actually fooled those priests?

"Oh when will Mamá and Papá be home?" she thought. "And what on earth will they say about what I have done?"

Chapter 6
Leaving in the Dark

Sara stood beside Yosef's bed in the darkness to make sure he was sleeping deeply. Only after she heard his rhythmic breathing did she make her way softly down the hall and open the door to her own room.

Carefully closing the door behind her, Sara put out the flame in the lamp before sitting down beside the trunk. What if the priests were still watching? What if they came back suddenly? All her senses were on alert.

"Devorah," Sara whispered. "Devorah, they're gone; you can come out now. Devorah, Devorah, are you all right?" she asked worriedly.

The orphan girl sat up with a groan, and brushed the arm of a woolen cloak from her face.

"That was close," Sara said, as she helped Devorah stand up and step out of the trunk. "One of the priests started sticking his hand into the trunk! I was so scared that he was going to find you," she said breathlessly.

Devorah pushed her hair out of her eyes, and flung her thin arms around Sara's neck.

"Thank you so much," she sobbed, hugging Sara tightly. "If you hadn't helped me, I would be on my way to an orphanage by now, and there would be no way for me to live as a Jew."

"I'm glad I could help you get away from those priests, my child," Sara said, mimicking their way of talking. She smiled at her new friend.

"So am I." Devorah smiled back and

tried to smooth the wrinkles out of her faded dress. "And Sara?" she asked hesitantly, twisting her hands together.

"What?" Sara asked, frowning slightly when she saw the anxious look on Devorah's face.

"You've already done so much for me, and I can't believe I'm going to ask you this... but, do you think your parents have decided to take me with you when you leave tomorrow?" Devorah asked hopefully.

Sara smiled, and wrapped an arm around Devorah's shoulders. "That's just why they're not here now. They went to speak to..." she began to say, when suddenly they heard strange, harsh voices in the hallway below!

Devorah looked fearfully at Sara. "Oh no," she whispered. "Do you think the priests came back?" she asked, her lips trembling.

Sara pushed Devorah back towards the trunk. "Quick, get in," she urged, covering Devorah once again with clothing. "I'll be right back," Sara whispered. "Don't make a sound."

Walking softly into the hallway, Sara strained her ears, listening as the voices grew louder. Peering over the bannister, she breathed a sigh of relief when she saw Mamá and Papá had returned.

"Mamá, Papá, you're back," Sara cried joyfully, hurrying down the stairs. She was simply bursting to tell her parents everything that had happened! Sara ran toward them, stopping suddenly when she saw two soldiers standing behind her parents.

"It's all right, Sara," Mamá assured her, seeing the frightened look that crossed her daughter's face. "Devorah has run away, and the soldiers are here to make sure we don't try to take her with us without permission. Papá's friend was unable to help, I'm sorry."

Sara sensed there was more. She looked up at her father, waiting.

Papá cleared his throat. "Just to make sure we don't break any rules, we must leave Cordoba tonight rather than tomorrow morning. These soldiers are here to escort us," he explained, wrapping an arm around Sara's shoulders.

"Oh," Sara said, "But I wanted to say goodbye to Raquel and all my other friends!"

"I wish you could," Papá answered grimly. "But it's impossible now. I'm not sorry we tried to help the daughter of my old friend, Don Isaac, and I hope Devorah finds another family to help her."

Calmly, Papá picked up a lamp and led the soldiers up the stairs. Mamá and Sara trailed behind him.

"Where are all your things?" the soldier asked harshly. "We don't have all night!"

"My wife's trunk and mine are in here," Papá said, motioning towards his bedroom.

The soldier looked at the trunks that the priests had so recently rummaged through. "Why aren't these packed?" the soldier demanded, stomping on some of the clothing that the priests had thrown on the floor.

"I have no idea," Papá said, a frown puckering his brow, as he put the lamp down on one of the dressers and bent to pick up the items.

"Two priests came here earlier looking for an orphan who had run away," Sara explained, clinging to her mother's side. "It must have been Devorah. They looked through all our trunks before they left. That's why the clothing is all over the floor."

"What are you talking about? What priests?" the soldier asked, as Mamá and Papá looked questioningly at Sara.

"They came here while you were in charge?" Papá murmured quietly, the worried look in his eyes matching the one in his wife's.

"It's true," the second soldier said. "The priests from the orphanage were looking for some girl earlier this evening. They checked these Jews' trunks to see if they were hiding her. Obviously, she wasn't here."

"Good," the first soldier replied. "That means we don't need to waste time checking these trunks again. Well," he snarled at Papá. "What are you waiting for? Get these things packed, and be quick about it."

"Sarita, please wake your brother, and help him get ready to leave," Mamá said, as she and Papá hurriedly re-packed their things under the glaring eyes of the soldiers.

"Hey, Tomás, follow her and make sure she doesn't try anything," Sara heard one of the soldiers say, as she opened Yosef's door.

"Yosef, Yosef," she whispered, bending over her sleeping brother, and smoothing the curls off his forehead.

"Wake up Yosef," Sara said, as Yosef rolled over and opened his eyes. "Mamá and Papá are back, and we need to get ready to leave now," she explained forcing herself to smile as Yosef yawned, and rubbed his eyes sleepily.

"But why are we leaving in the dark?" Yosef asked, as Sara helped him sit up.

"It will be more fun that way," Sara answered, handing him his clothes. "Now get dressed quickly."

Soon the little boy was ready. Sara picked up the lamp with one hand and held on to Yosef with the other.

"Go into Mamá and Papá's room," she instructed her brother, as they walked into the hall, the soldier following them. "I'll be there in just a minute. Go on."

Yosef looked fearfully at the soldier standing behind them, before letting go of his sister's hand and running down the hallway to their parents' room. The soldier walked behind him.

Sara put the lamp down on one of the

hall tables. The soldiers had forgotten about her for the moment. "How can I ask Mamá and Papá what to do about Devorah without the soldiers hearing me?" she wondered, opening the door to her room, and walking over to her trunk.

"And if the soldiers find Devorah, she will have to go to the orphanage, and we will all surely be punished," Sara agonized. She was afraid to say a word to her friend in the trunk.

"Come on, hurry up," one of the soldiers called from the other room.

"I'm almost finished," Sara replied, picking up some clothing from the floor and placing it in the trunk on top of where Devorah lay hidden. Sara thought about how courageously Devorah had acted... how she was willing to give up everything to remain Jewish. "Just like we are," Sara murmured to herself.

"No matter what," she thought, "I will never let them find Devorah. She *will* come with us tonight, even if she has to ride in my trunk the whole way!"

Sara had only minutes to think of a plan. As she glanced around her, she noticed the challah on her dresser. How wonderful! She placed whatever bread was left into the trunk where Devorah could reach it. Now it was time for the hard part. Devorah would need air.

"Hashem, please help me," Sara whispered. What could she use to make a hole in the heavy trunk? Suddenly, Sara remembered something. She had cut the challah with a knife not long ago. Where was it?

Frantically, the girl searched the dresser... no knife! Her palms felt sweaty and her head was beginning to ache. Wait! She had put it away so Yosef wouldn't touch it; she had put it in the drawer!

Quickly, Sara yanked open the drawer and closed her fingers around the precious knife. She bent down and scraped it across the edge of the trunk, over and over, until she had carved a few small dents.

Just then, the soldier came looking for her. "You must leave now," he said coldly.

Satisfied that Devorah would be able to breathe, Sara gently closed and locked her trunk. The air holes were hard to notice, but they were there.

"I'm ready," Sara said calmly to the soldier.

"What about all that?" the soldier asked Sara, pointing to the pile of discarded items that still lay on her bed.

"My trunk is full," Sara said bravely. "I can't fit anything else inside."

"Fine," the soldier said. "Let's go," he added, motioning for Sara to take the trunk with her.

Groaning, Sara managed to push her trunk into the hallway, just as Papá was walking out of Yosef's room, balancing his son's trunk on his shoulder. "Sarita, I'll get that," Papá said, grabbing her trunk and pushing it down the hallway with his foot. "Whew, is this heavy," he muttered under his breath.

"All right, all right, you've got your things. Hurry up," the soldier ordered.

Struggling to help her mother carry one of the trunks down the stairs, Sara looked down the hallway where she and Yosef had played and spent so much time. Swallowing a lump in her throat, Sara looked at her mother, and saw that tears were glistening in Mamá's eyes.

"Good-bye house," Sara whispered sadly, as the soldiers opened the front door.

"Come on, hurry up," they barked, motioning everyone outside. "And just where do you think you're going?" One of the soldiers stood in Mamá's path as she walked toward the kitchen.

"I must take some food and supplies with us for our trip," Mamá insisted.

"All right, all right," the soldier said, as Mamá hurried into the kitchen. She quickly wrapped up some fruit, some bread, and the small piece of dough she would need to make the next batch of bread rise. Into a wooden barrel, she placed a month's supply of dried beans and chickpeas, flour, spices, vinegar, honey, a cone of sugar and a cone of salt for cooking on the ship.

After hoisting the heavy trunks and the barrel into the cart, Papá helped Mamá, Sara and Yosef climb inside. There was no turning back.

The soldiers mounted their fine horses and set off, one in front and one behind the departing family.

As the wagon pulled away, Sara twisted around for one last look at the home she so loved. Tears streaming down her face, she watched as the house of her childhood was swallowed by darkness and disappeared from view.

* * *

As the wagon tipped and swayed precariously, Mamá wrapped a protective arm around Sara's shoulder. "Papá and I are so proud of you," she whispered.

"You are," Sara asked, "Why?"

"Because you were so brave when those priests came to the house while Papá and I were away, and you took such good care of your brother," Mamá said.

"Poor Devorah," she added, lowering her voice another notch until it was barely audible. "I pray that Hashem is watching over her, wherever she is, and that she will find a way out of Spain."

"But Mamá," Sara started to whisper, when one of the soldiers drew alongside them. How much could he hear? It wasn't safe to tell her secret yet.

Shrinking back against her mother, Sara looked over at her trunk. As the cart swayed and bounced down the road, a smile suddenly broke out on Sara's face as she pictured Devorah inside, getting the ride of her life!

As the wagon circled up the street and passed the homes of those who had chosen to stay, Mamá lowered her head sadly. "They may be keeping their homes, but they are losing everything that gives meaning to their lives," she whispered under her breath.

Sara sat silently, absorbing her mother's words. She thought of everything they had left behind, all their furniture, their garden, Yosef's toys, her jewelry... Suddenly Sara gasped out loud, her mind swirling in disbelief. The challah plate! She had packed it so carefully in her trunk, but now, where was it?

Sara's thoughts flew back to the discarded clothing lying on her bed. In all the excitement, the plate was probably beneath the pile she left behind. "Oh, how could I have been so careless?" she moaned to herself. "Now the plate will never be mine – even if I do learn how to bake the perfect challah," she thought.

Sara straightened her shoulders and smiled bravely.

"I may not have the silver plate in my trunk, but I do have something... someone, even more valuable! Won't Mamá and Papá be surprised when they find out?"

Chapter 7
Last Goodbye

Sara and her family spent a long night of travel on their way to the port. The jostling cart made sleep almost impossible, but the soldiers pushed them onward. Only when the Mizrahis were hours away from their home did the soldiers leave them and head back toward Cordoba.

Exhausted, the family stopped by the side of the road so Papá could put on tefillin. They all said their morning brachot as the first rays of sunlight began to peek over the horizon. Watching the beautiful pink and gold rays brighten the sky, Sara's spirits brightened, too. Perhaps now would be the perfect time to tell her parents about Devorah.

"Shalom, friends!" A familiar voice broke into Sara's thoughts. It was her father's friend, Asher Diaz. As he drew alongside in his wagon, Sara could see his wife, Isabel, and their twin boys, David and Yonatán, crowded in the back with their trunks.

"Aleichem shalom," Sara's father answered. "I'm so glad to see you, Asher.

This sad trip will be much easier to bear if we travel together."

"We'd be glad of your company too. The boys were always such good friends."

And so it was arranged. As the two families made their way to the Bay of Cadiz, it was amazing to see the hundreds of other Jews jamming the roads and crossing the fields, ready to board the waiting ships and begin a new life.

Hardship and despair were all around them. Trunks and bundles fell and were lost. Some people became sick, and others tried to help them.

Good Spanish citizens watched the struggles of the Jewish families with sorrow. "Why don't you give up being Jewish? Become just like us and stay," they urged from the side of the road.

"This is terrible," Asher Diaz muttered. "Everyone's spirits are so low. We don't want any Jews to change their minds and give up their faith now!"

Sara's father nodded. "Some singing will help, I'm sure. Let's try it!"

Yosef, David and Yonatán joined right in with their favorite songs, and Señora Diaz gave Sara a tambourine to liven things up. One by one, the heartbroken Jews around them joined in, their heads held a little higher, their hearts filling with hope for the future.

For the first time, Sara stopped thinking about all she left behind. Their beautiful home in Cordoba seemed like a lovely, but fading dream. Her worry over Devorah and her excitement about the long journey occupied all her waking thoughts.

With three little boys around all day, Sara felt it was unsafe to talk about Devorah's hiding place. What if one of the children let it slip at the wrong time? As soon as they boarded the ship, she would tell her parents. Sara couldn't wait to put the responsibility for Devorah firmly on her father and mother's grown up shoulders.

"My friend must be fainting from the heat," worried Sara. "I must get her some water." That night, after the adults had all fallen asleep, Sara unlocked her trunk, lifted the lid just a crack, and shook Devorah awake.

The girls both understood the need for silence and secrecy. Without a word, Sara slipped two skins full of water into the trunk. Devorah clutched her friend's hand for just a moment to let her know she was fine, and grateful for the water.

As they neared the harbor, Sara inhaled the salty, fishy ocean smell. They turned the corner, and straight ahead stood the tall ships that would be their home in the weeks to come. Tomorrow was Tisha B'Av, the deadline for all Jews to leave Spain.

Sailors scurried about, preparing the

ships. Jewish families, carrying their meager belongings, tried to round up their children. Newborn babies cried lustily, and old folks, reluctant to leave, wailed as they boarded the ships. What noise and confusion!

The next few hours went by quickly as the Mizrahi Family prepared for life on board ship. They unloaded their trunks, and Papá traded the ox and cart for some blankets. Mamá baked some flatbread over an open fire and bought fruits and vegetables in the local market.

Not for a second did they have any privacy, so Sara said nothing about the extra passenger hiding among her belongings. They watched as their trunks were loaded into the ship, Sara holding her breath as her trunk, with Devorah inside, was put down with a bump on the deck.

Sara boarded the ship, aware that these were her last footsteps on Spanish soil.

"When we get off the ship, my feet will be walking on a whole new land," she thought.

Yosef could barely stand still. The harbor was the most exciting place he had ever seen. Sara took him by the hand and made him finish the *huevos haminados* that Mamá had given him to eat for breakfast.

"Sarita, where did Papá and Mamá go?" he asked, looking up at the dirty white sails that billowed noisily in the breeze.

"They're below deck, arranging our living quarters," Sara murmured distractedly, "I hope Devorah is all right in there," Sara worried to herself. "I've got to get down there soon and slip her more food..."

"Sarita, look," Yosef pointed towards a group of Jews slowly walking past the harbor, as bells began to chime faintly in the distance. Yosef waved to them in his friendly way, but not one of them waved back to the little boy.

"Sara, why won't they wave back?" Yosef asked, a puzzled look on his face.

Sara patted her brother's head comfortingly. "Don't worry Yosef," she said, watching as they walked around the corner and disappeared from view. "'Those poor Jews have to go and hear the priests speak. They act like they don't see us, because they've decided to stay in Spain and pretend that they are no longer Jewish," she explained to her brother.

"Oh," Yosef said. "Is that why they look so sad?" he asked.

Sara nodded, and lifted her head proudly. "That's right Yosef," she said. "And they will be sad forever because they are living a lie."

Yosef stood silently for a moment, absorbing his sister's words. "But we won't live like that, so that's why we're leaving today," he said. "Because we will never give up Torah and mitzvot, right?"

"That's right," Sara smiled at her brother. "Torah and mitzvot are more precious than gold. Mamá and Papá would rather leave Spain and have to start over in a new country rather than stop living as Jews. I'm so proud of them."

Yosef smiled back at Sara. "So am I," he said.

Sara put her arm around Yosef the moment the ship began to move, its sails billowing in the wind. The Mizrahi Family and thousands of Jews who had lived in Spain for generations were off on a journey to the unknown, and nothing would ever be the same.

* * *

Sara and Yosef made their way through the throngs of people crowded together on one of the lower decks of the ship. "Sara, Yosef, please come wash and make *Ha'motzi*. I want you put something more in your stomachs so you won't get seasick," Mamá said. "I was worried you wouldn't be able to find me," she added, as Sara and Yosef used the bucket standing in the corner near the wall to wash their hands.

Sara made the bracha and took a bite of the last of Mamá's delicious bread. "Papá told us exactly how to find you down here," she said, "He's up on deck talking to some other men about when we will land. They think it will take us at least three weeks to reach our new home."

Mamá nodded. "That's true. So let's make our little corner of this ship as comfortable as possible." Mamá unfolded one of the blankets they had brought on board.

"Sarita, help me hang this so we have some privacy," Mamá said, handing Sara one corner, and draping the other corner over the rope that separated their living quarters from that of their neighbors'.

As Sara tried to help, she noticed how pale her mother looked. Maybe the rocking motion of the ship was making Mamá dizzy. "As soon as she feels better," thought Sara, "I will tell her about Devorah. Meanwhile, I'd better get some food and water to my friend."

"Mamá, may I go look around for a while?" she asked, carefully hiding a small jug of water and some food behind the wide sleeves of her dress.

"All right, but be careful," Mamá instructed. She and Yosef began to set up sleeping pallets on the floor for everyone. "And Sarita, don't go too far."

"Yes, Mamá," Sara said, breaking into a fast trot as soon as Mamá and Yosef were out of sight.

Soon she reached the staircase that led to the upper and lower decks of the ship. Looking around to be sure no on saw her, Sara began to creep down the stairs, peering through the gloom. Where would all the trunks be stored for the rest of the trip?

Finally, she saw an enormous doorway leading to the hold of the ship.

Stepping cautiously inside, Sara began searching for her trunk among all the others. "Ahh," she yelped as a huge rat ran right in front of her and scurried off into the darkness. Watching where she stepped, Sara carefully made her way around dozens of boxes and trunks, before finally spying hers in the corner.

"Oh, thank G-d no one put any other trunks on top of it," she whispered, running over and knocking on the lid.

"Devorah, it's me, Sara," she called, setting down the food and fumbling with the lock. "I'm going to open the trunk. Don't be afraid," she said, pushing open the top of the trunk with a grunt.

"Sara?" Devorah croaked, licking lips that were parched with thirst. Sara helped her sit up. "Are you all right?" she asked. "Here, drink some water." She held the jug carefully and poured some water into Devorah's mouth.

Whispering the bracha, Devorah gulped down the water, and wiped her mouth on the back of her hand. "I ran out of food and water yesterday," she said. "I tried to save it, but I was too thirsty and hungry."

Sara helped her friend stand and step out of the trunk. Devorah could barely walk after all that time in the small space.

"I'm so sorry that I couldn't come sooner," Sara said, handing Devorah some fruit and the delicious *huevos haminados*. "But my parents still don't know you are here..."

Devorah threw her arms around Sara's neck. "You are so brave, Sara!" she declared. "I can never repay you for what you have done!" She bit into one of the eggs and sighed contentedly.

"You are pretty brave yourself," Sara said, hugging her friend.

"Sara, what's wrong?" Devorah asked,

"Why do you look so sad?"

Sara tried to smile. "I'm all right, Devorah," she said. "I'm just upset because I forgot all about the challah plate when the soldiers came back with my parents. We had to leave in such a hurry, and I think I took it out of my trunk. Now it's lost forever..."

Devorah grinned suddenly and stood up, motioning for Sara to do the same. Reaching deep down inside the trunk, Devorah smiled and pulled out -- the challah plate!

"Our challah plate!" Sara cried, grabbing the plate out of Devorah's hands. "But how on earth..." she started to say.

"I wondered what was making that wagon ride so uncomfortable," Devorah laughed. "I didn't know what I was lying on, until I managed to reach under me, and there it was," she said. "You didn't take it out of your trunk after all!"

Sara hugged Devorah. "This is so wonderful," she said. "Remember, it's all thanks to you that the soldiers didn't get it to begin with!"

Devorah hugged Sara back. "And thanks to you, the priests didn't get me, either!" she declared.

* * *

"Sarita, there you are," Mamá said, relief flooding her face, as Sara poked her head around the blanket. "Please don't walk around the ship by yourself for such a long time again. I was starting to get worried. Papá is looking for you."

"I'm sorry Mamá," Sara said. Noticing that Yosef had fallen asleep on one of the pallets on the floor, Sara gently covered him with a blanket.

Mamá turned around suddenly, and began coughing into a bucket.

"Are you all right Mamá?" Sara asked worriedly.

Mamá wiped her mouth on a handkerchief. "I'm just feeling a little queasy, Sara. It's probably seasickness. As soon as I'm used to the swaying of the ship, I hope it will go away."

Sara nodded and poured her mother a cup of water. "Here, maybe this will help you feel better."

Mamá smiled weakly at her daughter. "Thank you, Sarita, but you know that I and all the other adults are fasting. Today is the saddest day of the Jewish calendar. Tisha B'Av was when the first and second Batei Mikdash were destroyed."

"And now this sad thing is happening to us on the very same day," Sara mused.

She glanced at her mother out of the corner of her eye. Mamá's face was pale, and she shivered, clutching a cloak tightly around her shoulders.

"If I tell Mamá about Devorah, it will worry her," Sara thought. "And I shouldn't worry her when she is ill – or Papá either – so I better not tell anyone about Devorah just yet."

"Sarita, here you are," Papá said, as he pushed aside the blanket.

Sara nodded, and pointed to where Yosef lay sleeping. Papá nodded back, and walked over to where Mamá sat. "How are you feeling?" he asked with concern.

Mamá tried to smile. "Better, I think," she said, before turning and coughing into the bucket again.

"You must lie down and rest," Papá urged. "Close your eyes."

"But I need to make a meal for when the fast day is over," Mamá said, trying to push herself up.

"Don't worry Mamá, I can make some

food for everyone, I think," Sara said as she tucked a blanket around her mother.

"Oh Sarita, what would I do without you?" Mamá said. She closed her eyes wearily.

"Will Mamá be all right?" Sara whispered. Papá nodded.

"Mamá will be fine," he reassured his daughter. "It seems like a bad case of seasickness. There's not much I can do for that, but G-d willing, in a few days she'll feel better."

"Really, Papá?" Sara asked anxiously.

"Really, Sarita," Papá smiled.

"Good," Sara said. "And I'll make sure to do everything I can so Mamá can rest and get well."

Papá smiled at Sara and kissed her. "Thank you, Sarita," he said. "Mamá and I are very grateful to have you as our daughter."

Sara tried to smile back at her father, but her stomach felt tight with worry. Would she really be able to take proper care of Papá, Mamá, Yosef and Devorah, all by herself?

Chapter 8

Danger on Board

Early the next morning, Sara quietly dressed behind the blanket, and said her morning *tefillot* while the rest of her family lay sleeping. Carrying her shoes in one hand, and some food and water in the other, Sara tiptoed quietly around the many people who lay wrapped in blankets.

Reaching the hallway, she bent over to slip on her shoes, and suddenly lost her balance, nearly tripping on the elderly woman who lay by the door.

"Watch what you're doing!" the woman hissed grumpily. "Oh, I beg your pardon," Sara murmured, her face reddening with embarrassment.

Running over to the staircase, Sara started to make her way down to the hold. She was almost there, when suddenly she heard loud, harsh voices below her.

"Sailors!" she whispered to herself, looking around frantically for a place to hide.

"I hate the early morning watch," one of the sailors complained.

Looking above her, Sara spied a small doorway. "Please don't be locked," she prayed silently, as she ran up the narrow stairs. Pulling on the handle, she slipped behind the door, just as two large men trudged past her hiding place!

"Hey, did you hear something?" the sailor asked, stopping right in front of the door where Sara was hiding. Sara held her breath; sweat trickled down her face.

"No, I didn't hear anything," the other sailor said impatiently. "Come on!"

"I'm telling you, I heard something," the first sailor insisted, as they continued walking up the stairs.

"You probably heard some rats running around looking for breakfast," Sara heard the other sailor reply, as their footsteps grew fainter and fainter. Breathing a sigh of relief, Sara slipped out from behind the door, and ran swiftly down the stairs. "That was close," she whispered.

"Devorah, it's Sara," she called, as she made her way to the trunk.

"Sara, good morning," Devorah said, poking her head up from behind a large stack of boxes.

"Good morning," Sara replied, hugging her friend, and handing her the food.

"Did you sleep all right? Is it really safe for you to be down here?" Sara asked, looking around the dark, musty hold.

Devorah frowned. "Sailors were in here yesteday," she said worriedly. "They are going through people's trunks and stealing whatever they can. I managed to stay out of their way, but I'm going to need a second hiding place when they get to this corner."

"I must tell my father about this," Sara gasped. "But first, let's make another place for you to hide."

The two girls scurried between the trunks until they found an empty barrel lying on its side. "Those sailors must have emptied whatever was in here," Devorah said. "If I have to leave your trunk, I'll just crawl inside."

"Good," Sara said. "But just to be safe, we should come up with a signal so you'll know when I'm here and it's safe to come out."

Devorah nodded. "Absolutely," she

agreed. "Maybe you should knock on the floor twice," she suggested.

Sara nodded, her eyes brightening. "And then I'll say '*Shema Yisrael Hashem Elokeinu*'," she said.

"And I'll knock back three times, and say '*Hashem Echad*'," Devorah cried.

Sara clapped her hands together in satisfaction. "Perfect!" she declared, as Devorah made a bracha and began eating her breakfast.

"My mother isn't feeling well," Sara said, sitting close to her friend. "So I couldn't tell her or Papá about you right now. I'm going to be busy making all our meals, doing the washing, and looking after my little brother until my mother feels better. I'll only be able to bring you food and water in the morning before everyone wakes up. I hope that's all right."

Devorah smiled. "That's fine, Sara. I'll

save some of this food for later. I only wish that I could help you. I feel so useless just sitting down here. I really hope your mother feels better soon," she said.

Sara nodded. "So do I."

* * *

Poking her head around the doorway, Sara checked that no one was outside, before waving good-bye to Devorah, and starting to creep back up the stairs. "Oh no, not again,"

she groaned softly, as she heard voices coming from above. Turning around, she started hurrying back down to the hold, when suddenly she heard her father's voice rise above the others.

"I know it isn't right for the Captain to ask for more money when we've already paid twice the usual amount, but what choice do we have?" Papá said. "We have to protect our families and keep them safe until we reach the Ottoman Empire."

Sara peered around the winding staircase, her eyes widening when she saw her father standing next to Asher Diaz and two other men she didn't recognize.

Asher Diaz shook his head. "If we pay him again, he'll just keep demanding more and more," he said. "We barely have any money left now. When will it stop, Moshe?" he asked.

"And what will we do when all our money is gone, and the Captain keeps demanding we pay more?" a tall, quiet man asked. "What then?"

Sara hated to interrupt, but she had to warn the men about what was going on in the hold. "Papá," she said softly. Her father turned to her with a worried look. "What is it, Sarita?"

She took a deep breath before answering. "I found out that our belongings in the hold aren't safe. The sailors are taking whatever they please from our trunks."

Papá sighed. "I was afraid of that," he said softly. "But we don't have any choices right now. We are at the mercy of the captain and his crew."

"I don't like this," Asher muttered. "We've been at sea for one day, and already we're being treated like..." his voice trailed off as he sputtered angrily.

Papá put up his hand. "Don't let this bother you too much," he said calmly. "We must have faith that this will all work out, but right now, we need to stay safe and forget about our belongings. Our wives and children and parents are counting on us," he said, starting to walk up to the deck where the rabbi led the morning tefillot.

Sara watched as the two men followed her father. "Asher, are you coming?" the tall man called over his shoulder.

"Yes, yes, I'm coming," Asher muttered, following the men up the stairs.

Standing silently for a moment, Sara thought about what she had just heard.

"If the sailors discover Devorah is on board, they'll want even more money from us. How will all this end?" she wondered despairingly.

"We left a land of danger, and this ship is full of danger, too. When will we finally be safe?"

* * *

As the first week flew by, Sara faithfully

woke up early every morning to slip Devorah some food and water, before spending the rest of the day taking care of Yosef, and preparing meals for her family up on deck. Señora Diaz helped Sara make flatbread and cook the simple foods they needed.

Papá did everything he could to make Mamá more comfortable, but by their first erev Shabbat on the ship, Mamá still lay on her pallet, too weak from nausea to get up.

So, Sara began checking and washing white beans for a Shabbat dish that could be cooked before Shabbat and eaten cold the next day. "I hope this tastes good," Sara thought, as she added onions, spices and honey to the pot.

All the families on board were trying to do something special for Shabbat, shaking out blankets, washing clothing, and tidying up as best they could. When the sun began to sink lower and lower on the horizon, Mamá and the other women lit the Shabbat flames. The men and boys sang the Shabbat tefillot together, and at that moment, Sara felt all the holiness of the day as much as when they celebrated it in their beautiful home in Spain.

During the meal that night, Sara managed to slip away and sneak downstairs to see Devorah. She knocked twice on the floor and whispered, "*Shema Yisrael Hashem Elokeinu.*" Then she waited to hear three knocks in reply and Devorah's soft voice answering, "*Hashem Echad.*"

"Shabbat Shalom," Sara said. She pulled out some flatbread and the food she had cooked for Devorah to taste. "How is it?" she asked.

Devorah washed her hands, made the bracha and took a bite of bread, then tasted the beans. "Everything's delicious, Sara!" she exclaimed.

"Are you sure you're not just saying

that because you're hungry?" Sara asked.

"Are you sure it's the first time you've cooked for Shabbat by yourself?" Devorah replied. The two girls giggled softly and sat on the trunk, side by side.

"I'm sorry that you have to spend Shabbat down here, all by yourself," Sara apologized. Devorah shook her head, as she ate more of the food Sara had brought her.

"This is one of my happiest Shabbat meals ever," she started to say, when suddenly she and Sara heard the door creak open, and harsh voices filled the room. There was no time to get into the barrel. What could they do?

"Quick, hide over here," Devorah whispered in Sara's ear, pulling her friend back into the corner behind the trunk.

"But your food," Sara whispered back, pointing to where Devorah's little meal sat. "They might see it."

Devorah shook her head violently. "Leave it! It's too late now," she whispered as they saw two large figures stepping between the boxes and trunks.

"Won't these Jews be in for a surprise when they land and find that all the valuables they managed to smuggle out of Spain have been taken home by our beloved Captain," one voice hissed with an evil laugh.

"Absolutely," a second voice agreed. The sounds of trunks being pried open, and boxes being shaken reached the girls' ears. "But remember, the rest of the crew can't know about this, or we'll have to share the spoils with everyone, got it?"

"Got it," the first voice said.

Poking their heads around the trunk, Sara and Devorah watched in horror as two sailors rummaged through several trunks and boxes, stuffing what little they found into a sack. As one of the sailors turned suddenly towards their corner, Sara crawled back behind the trunk, and felt something run over her fingers. Gasping, she pulled her hand up to her throat, as a rat scurried off into a dark corner.

"Who's there?" the first sailor called, whipping around, the lantern in his hand making his face glow darkly. "I said, who's there? Come out and show yourself!"

Devorah and Sara clung to each other, trembling as they heard the sailor's heavy footsteps come closer and closer. "I said, who's there? Aggh, rats!" the sailor yelped. He jumped backwards suddenly and lost his balance. With a crash, he landed right on top of a stack of boxes.

"Oohh, oohh, that was a good one," the second sailor whooped with laughter, as his friend angrily picked himself up. "Quiet, you fool," the first sailor hissed. "We're lucky I didn't drop the lantern and burn up both of us."

"Come out and show yourself... what did you expect the rats to do, obey?" the second sailor wiped tears from his eyes.

"I said, quiet," the first sailor barked. "Come on, we got enough for one night, not that there is much to get. We'll come back tomorrow. Let's go."

Sara and Devorah listened as the door creaked shut behind the sailors, before standing up. "Whew, that was close," Devorah said. "Are you all right?" she asked.

Sara nodded, her knees still shaking. "I can't believe I almost got us caught," she said weakly. "I'm so sorry, Devorah."

Devorah hugged Sara. "I would have done the same thing if a rat ran over my hand," she said. "Come, sit down. Have some water; it will make you feel better."

Sara shook her head. "You need that water more than I do, remember?" she said.

Sara took some deep breaths, as the feeling slowly began to return to her legs. "I can't believe you're used to this going on all the time. I was so scared."

Devorah shook her head. "Don't worry, I'm scared every time they come. They are getting closer to the trunk now. I better take up hiding in the barrel from now on."

"My father said there's nothing that can be done," Sara said sadly. "Just take care of yourself, Devorah."

Devorah smiled bravely. "Don't worry Sara. I'm sure that Hashem will protect me."

Sara looked around at all the trunks the thieving sailors still had left to go through. "Oh, no!" Sara cried, jumping up suddenly.

"Sara what is it?" Devorah asked, jumping up also. "What's wrong?"

"The challah plate!" Sara declared, throwing open the lid of her trunk and clutching the plate in her hands. "Oh, what if those wicked sailors find it? I'd better take it upstairs with me."

"Don't do that," Devorah said. "What if the sailors start going through everyone's things upstairs, too? It will be safer here," she said. "I'll keep the plate with me at all times, Sara, honest."

"Thank you, Devorah," Sara said, clutching the plate and tracing the beautifully embossed border with her finger. Softly, Sara began to sing the *Shalom Alecheim* her father always sang on Friday nights.

Smiling, Devorah linked arms with Sara. The two girls sat in the darkness, whispering songs of joy, picturing what Shabbat would be like in their new home across the ocean.

* * *

"Doctor Mizrahi, please, Doctor Mizrahi," someone whispered outside their curtain. Sara sat up sleepily and rubbed her eyes, as Papá jumped off his pallet and poked his head outside. "Yes, what is it, Señora?" he asked softly.

"Please, you must come," Sara heard a woman say desperately. "My mother is very ill. Her fever keeps climbing. Please hurry."

"In a moment, Señora," Papá said soothingly. "Let me first tell my wife. I'll be right there."

Sara watched as Papá quickly grabbed some cloths and a jug of cool water. He walked over to where Mamá lay.

"Moshe," Sara heard her mother ask. "Is everything all right? Are the children all right?"

"Yes, Mazal," Papá said. "The children are sleeping, but someone is ill, and I must try to help. I'll be back as soon as I can. Wake Sarita if you need anything," he said.

"I will, Moshe," Mamá answered.

Tiptoeing over to the curtain, Sara peered around it to see what was happening. She watched her father bend down next to an elderly woman who lay very still on some blankets on the floor. Smiling reassuringly at the woman, Papá checked her breathing, and placed a cool cloth on her forehead.

"Doctor, is there anything you can do?" the woman's daughter asked fearfully.

Papá shook his head sadly. "I'm sorry," he said. "Without any medicine, we can only keep her as cool and comfortable as possible," he said. "And say Tehillim."

The young woman put her head in her hands. Sara saw her lips moving in silent prayer, as tears fell onto the blanket that covered the old woman.

Crawling back to bed, Sara stared into the darkness for what felt like hours, before Papá finally pushed aside the curtain, and stepped inside.

"Papá," Sara called softly.

"Yes Sarita, what is it?" Papá asked, hurrying over to her pallet. "Are you feeling ill?" he asked worriedly, laying a hand across her forehead.

"No Papá," Sara shook her head. "Is, is that woman going to be all right?" she asked.

Papá sighed. "I just don't know, Sarita," he said softly. "She is in Hashem's hands, as we all are." Doctor Mizrahi kissed his daughter's forehead, and turned to go back to bed.

Sara lay on her hard pallet and closed her eyes. She listened to the creaking of the ship, the scratching of the rats, the sound of babies crying, and people coughing. "Oh, when will this long journey end?" she wondered, before falling into a deep, dreamless sleep.

Chapter 9
Journey's End

"Sarita," Mamá called out one morning after Papá and Yosef had left to say their morning tefillot with the other men and boys. Although Papá kept reassuring Sara that her mother would be fine, Mamá remained weak and pale, unable to care for the family.

"Yes Mamá," Sara answered, hurrying over to where Mamá still lay on her pallet. "Do you need anything?" she asked anxiously.

"Not right now, thank you," Mamá said. "Please tell me what day it is."

Sara looked at the little calendar that Papá and Yosef had made. "It's the 29th of Av, Mamá," she said.

Mamá pushed herself up on her elbows. "That means we've been at sea for about three weeks," she mused.

Sara nodded. "Papá said we should reach the port of Smryna tomorrow or the next day," she said, tucking a blanket around her mother's shoulders, and holding a cup of water to her lips.

Lying back down, Mamá smiled weakly at her daughter. "You've been so wonderful Sarita," she said softly, stroking her daughter's cheek lovingly. "I don't know how I would have survived this trip without all your help. I know cooking meals over an open fire on deck isn't easy, especially having to wait on the long lines for a turn. I'm so sorry that I can't do more."

Sara blushed, and bent down to kiss her mother's cheek. "I don't mind, Mamá," she said. "I just want you to feel better."

In truth, the little Sarita who had left

her comfortable life in Spain was not the same Sara who now had the responsibility for the hard work and care of so many people. Each morning, she secretly made her way to the hold, where she brought Devorah food and water. The girls were always afraid that the sailors would discover the hidden orphan, so their visits together were short.

Then Sara would clean her family's little corner of the ship and cook food up on deck when the weather was good. At first her flatbread was a bit lumpy, but when she had done it a few times, Papá and Yosef said it was just as good as Mamá's.

Papá relied on Sara completely. He was constantly busy, coming by to check on Mamá and hurrying off again. With so many people crammed into such a small and dirty space, sickness was all around them, and her father's skill as a doctor was in great demand. For that reason, a great part of her day was spent looking after Yosef. Her brother did have the company of other little boys on the ship, and Señor Diaz taught them their lessons, but when Yosef was hungry, scared, or hurt, he came running to Sara.

The rest of her time was spent caring for Mamá. Sara would gently wipe her

mother's forehead with a wet cloth,

encouraging her to drink and to try a bit of food. Sara washed the family's clothing as best she could in seawater, and her hands grew rough and sore from doing all the work that servants had done for her family in the past.

Sometimes, late at night, when Sara was too exhausted to sleep, she would throw a cloak over her shoulders and tiptoe up to the quiet deck. The sea was an endless black, and the sky twinkled with a thousand stars.

"Hashem, please help us reach our new home in safety," Sara would say, over and over. It was the only thing that mattered.

* * *

"Sara," Yosef called one morning, "guess what!"

"Shhhh," Sara said, putting a finger to her lips. "Mamá is trying to rest."

"Sorry, Mamá," Yosef whispered tugging on Sara's arm. "Come up on deck. We can see the port, and we're going to land soon."

"Already?" Sara said excitedly, before looking over at her mother. Opening her eyes, Mamá smiled. "Go on Sarita, I'll be fine," she said.

"Are you sure?" Sara asked.

"Yes, I'm sure," Mamá answered, with a wave of her hand. "Go."

Running upstairs, Sara and Yosef made their way through the throngs of people who had gathered on deck. "Sarita, Yosef, over here," they heard Señor Diaz call from where he stood next to the railing. "Look," he said, pointing to the faint outline of a dock that stood in the distance. "That's the port of Smryna. We should land in just a few hours."

Yosef bounced up and down excitedly.

"Isn't it great Sara?" he asked.

Sara stared silently at the horizon. The wind whipped through her long curly hair. Soon they would arrive, and her feet would step on the land of their new home. Sara swallowed as a lump rose in her throat.

"Sarita?" Yosef asked anxiously. "Sarita, are you all right?"

Looking down at her little brother, Sara smiled, and wrapped an arm around his shoulders. "I'm fine, Yosef," she said. "Just fine."

The first chance she got, Sara crept down to the hold to tell Devorah the news.

"We've only got a few hours before the sailors will be down here unloading the trunks."

Devorah's eyes lit up with excitement. "I never thought this day would come!"

The two girls hugged, and Sara helped Devorah back into the trunk, fastening the lid tightly.

"See you later," they whispered. Then Sara made her way back upstairs to help with the packing.

Finally the ship dropped anchor, and the rush began. Families hurried to gather their belongings and struggled to keep track of their impatient children.

Papá arranged for several of the men to move the passengers who were ill to shore first. As they waited their turn to leave, Sara and Yosef watched the sailors begin to unload the trunks and boxes from the hold.

Recognizing her trunk, Sara held her breath, as two sailors grabbed at the net, and pulled it down on the dock with a loud thump. Sara cringed, imagining how Devorah must feel being knocked around like that.

"Sarita, when do you think we'll finally get to go ashore and see our new home?" Yosef asked.

Sara shrugged. "I don't know," she said, shading her eyes from the glinting sunlight. "Look at all those people," she added, pointing to a large crowd that had gathered on the dock.

"They look just like us!" Yosef said excitedly. "They're Jews!"

Sara smiled down at her little brother. "They must be from the Turkish Jewish community," she said. "It's nice of them to welcome us to our new home."

Papá walked up behind his children, and wrapped an arm around their shoulders. "That's right Sarita," he said. "The tall man in the middle is Rabbi Yehuda Eskenas. He was in charge of helping us resettle here." .

* * *

"Shalom Alecheim, Doctor Mizrahi," Rabbi Eskenas called to them several hours later. He watched as Papá helped Mamá, Sara and Yosef climb out of the last rowboat, and stand on solid ground for the first time in weeks.

"Alecheim Shalom," Papá replied, shaking the rabbi's hand happily. "It's good to meet you face to face, Rabbi Eskenas. Thank you so much for all that you and your community have done for us."

Rabbi Eskenas smiled and shrugged.

"What did we do, after all? Managed to build some very simple housing; put up some tents and helped make some travel arrangements for our fellow Jews. Everything we did, you would have done for us. Besides, you're the ones who had the hardship of having to move," he said. "And now, thanks to the One Above, you're here, safe and sound."

Papá nodded. "This is my wife, Mazal, and these are our children, Sara and Yosef," he said, introducing his family to the rabbi.

Rabbi Eskenas smiled at Mamá and Sara, and tousled Yosef's hair. "My wife is at home, trying to make sure that everyone settles in comfortably. Come, let's use my wagon; you must be exhausted, and it will be quite a wait for the other carts to return."

Papá helped Mamá into the rabbi's wagon, and then walked over to show their papers to the officers standing on the dock next to the passengers' cargo. "It was a pleasure having you aboard, Doctor," one of the officers said mockingly, as he stood aside and watched Papá and Rabbi Eskenas take the trunks.

"Yes, the Captain wants us to thank you and your fellow shipmates for all your generous contributions to his worthy cause, our pockets," the second officer added with an evil laugh.

Papá and Rabbi Eskenas's eyes burned with anger, as they began loading the trunks onto the back of the wagon.

Sara clenched her hands angrily as she thought about the wicked captain and his crew. They had stolen everything they could from her parents and all the other passengers. As Papá helped her climb into the back of the wagon, Sara looked down at her trunk, and remembered her friend hiding inside, guarding the precious challah plate. "They didn't get everything," she whispered softly. "Not everything."

* * *

Looking around the bare front room of their temporary house, Sara helped her mother lie down on the blankets Papá had laid out in the corner. "Well, it's not much," Mamá said, coughing softly. "But it will do quite nicely for now. Baruch Hashem we have a roof over our heads, and we are all together."

"And we are close to the communal oven," Sara declared, glancing out the door. "I won't have far to go to do the baking."

"My goodness, what is in this trunk of yours Sarita?" Papá groaned, as he and Yosef dropped her trunk in the corner and wiped the sweat from their foreheads. "I'm amazed Rabbi Eskenas's wagon is still in one piece," he added.

Sara's heart began to thump wildly. How would her parents feel about the risk she had taken to save her friend?

"Papá," Sara said hesitantly.

"Yes Sarita, what is it?" Papá said, taking the jug of water Yosef handed him.

"What... what would you think about someone who helped a fellow Jew escape Spain because she didn't want to give up Torah and mitzvot?" Sara asked, twisting her hands nervously.

Papá handed the jug back to Yosef, and wiped his mouth on a handkerchief. "I would think that was a very brave person," he said slowly, looking at his wife, and raising his eyebrows. "But why are you asking such a question?"

Smiling with relief, Sara ran over to her trunk, and threw open the lid. "This is why my trunk is so heavy, Papá," she cried, helping Devorah stand and step out of the trunk.

"What in the world," Mamá said weakly, as Papá and Yosef's mouths dropped open in disbelief. "Devorah? How

on earth did you get into Sara's trunk?" Papá asked.

Staring down at her feet, Devorah's face turned red. "It was all because of Sara's bravery!" she declared.

"Sarita, what's going on?" Mamá asked, as Sara turned towards her stunned parents.

"Devorah came while you and Papá were out," Sara explained. "I know I wasn't supposed to let anyone in, but then I heard those nasty soldiers coming, and I just couldn't let them find her..." she said, spreading her hands out in front of her.

"You made such an important decision without telling us?" Papá asked, closing the lid of the trunk and motioning for Devorah to sit down.

"There wasn't time, Papá," Sara said desperately, turning towards her father. "You weren't there, and when you came back those soldiers were always with us. I was afraid they might overhear me, and make Devorah go to the orphanage and punish us because I hid her in my trunk."

Mamá and Papá looked at each other. "Why didn't you tell us once we were on board the ship?" Mamá asked.

Sara looked down at her hands. "You were so ill, Mamá," she said. "And Papá was so busy helping all the other passengers that I didn't want to worry you. And then the Captain began demanding more money, and I worried that if anyone knew I had smuggled Devorah on board, the Captain would make Papá pay even more," Sara said.

Mamá and Papá looked at one another again. "You knew about the Captain's demands?" Papá said slowly.

Sara nodded. "I overheard you speaking with Señor Diaz, and some other men, Papá," she said. "So I brought food and water to Devorah every morning in the hold. I was sure that I was doing what you would want me to do," she said anxiously, watching her parent's faces. "I was sure that I was doing the right thing."

Papá's eyes glowed with pride as he wrapped an arm around Sara's shoulders. "You were exactly right," he declared, hugging his daughter tightly.

Mamá smiled and nodded her head. "I'm so proud of you," she said softly, tears welling in her gentle eyes. "You took care of all this yourself and ran our temporary household on the ship while I was ill. You really are growing up."

Sara smiled, and stared down at her feet. "I just did what you and Papá taught me to do," she said softly, "to always help a fellow Jew."

Devorah stood up, and walked over to

Sara. "Thank you Sara," she said, throwing her arms around Sara's shoulders.

Sara felt so relieved that her parents approved of all she had done. It was as if a huge weight had been lifted from her shoulders. Suddenly, she grinned and said, "Well, Devorah, it's time for one more surprise, isn't it?"

Devorah reached into the trunk, pulled out the challah plate and waved it triumphantly over her head. "I told you I wouldn't let anything happen to it," she said with a smile.

Mamá and Papá stared at the plate, and then at Sara. "How did you two manage to save it?" Papá asked, looking amazed.

"I thought the soldiers found it and took it away before we boarded the ship," Mamá said, as Sara handed her mother the one family treasure that had escaped the clutches of the wicked Ferdinand and

Isabella. "Not only did you help Devorah escape Spain, but you managed to save our challah plate as well," she murmured, her eyes shining with pride.

Throwing her arms around Devorah's shoulders, Sara grinned at her parents. "Not just me, Mamá," she said proudly. "We!"

Chapter 10
New Beginnings

Very early Friday morning, Sara rolled over and groaned softly, quickly reciting the *Modeh Ani.* Every muscle in her body ached from the hours of helping Papá set up the house. "This must be how Mamá feels after cleaning for Pesach," she muttered softly, stretching her arms over her head.

Walking behind the curtain that Papá had tacked up in one corner of the room, Sara pulled on her clothes, and brushed her hair. The sound of deep breathing came from the corner where Devorah lay curled up on a pallet. Sara smiled to herself as she said her morning prayers.

Tiptoeing over to the fireplace, Sara

worked on the glowing embers until a small blaze was burning steadily. Picking up two buckets from their place next to the door, Sara walked to the communal well that stood behind the row of houses. She filled each bucket to the brim with cool water and walked slowly so as not to spill any on the dusty ground.

The sun was just beginning to peak over the horizon, and Sara watched the slanting rays begin to brighten the roofs of the huts. "Good morning, sun! What a lovely day to prepare for the first Shabbat in our new home!"

Setting the buckets down gently next to the door, Sara pushed stray strands of hair out of her eyes, and wiped her forehead with the back of her hand.

"Good morning, good morning," Papá boomed, as he and Yosef walked in from their morning tefillot.

"Good morning Papá," Sara said, ladling some water into the large pot that hung above the fire in the hearth. "Your breakfast will be ready in a moment," she added, dipping a cup into one of the buckets and handing it to Yosef. "How does Mamá feel this morning?" she asked anxiously.

Now that they were no longer on the ship, Sara just couldn't understand why Mamá wasn't better yet.

"She is doing fine, Baruch Hashem, but it will be few weeks before she is completely well," he answered. "Come, Yosef," Papá held out his hand. "Your Torah class with Señor Diaz will start soon. I don't want you to be late." Yosef nodded, yawning as Sara handed him some lunch wrapped in a kerchief.

"Do you need me to pick up anything at the market on my way home for Shabbat?" Papá asked. "I am going to check on some of my new patients this morning, but I shouldn't be too long."

Sara shook her head. "No thank you, Papá," she said. "Señora Diaz stopped by yesterday to see how Mamá was feeling, and offered to pick up everything we need for Shabbat when she goes to the market this morning."

"That was very kind of her," Papá smiled. "We're blessed to have such helpful friends." Papá and Yosef waved good-bye, softly closing the door behind them.

Sara glanced over to where Mamá lay sleeping. "Why is Mamá still feeling ill?" she wondered, as she poured a glass of goat's milk. "Her seasickness should be gone by now, shouldn't it?"

"Mamá?" Sara called, knocking softly on the door. "Mamá, are you awake? I've brought you something to drink."

"Come in Sarita," Mamá called weakly.

Opening the door, Sara squinted into the semi-darkness of the room, and carefully handed her mother the milk. "How are you feeling Mamá?" she asked, walking over to the tiny window, and pushing aside the blanket that served as a curtain.

"Better, thank G-d," Mamá answered, blinking her eyes against the sunlight that streamed across the room. "I was hoping I would be able to get up today and help you prepare for Shabbat, but Papá said I need a few more days off my feet."

Sara kissed Mamá's cheek, and tucked the blankets more securely around her mother. "Please don't worry," she said. "Devorah and I will take care of everything."

Mamá looked proudly at her daughter and smiled. "I know you will, Sarita. I'm so proud of my grown up girl."

Sara blushed, and took the empty glass that Mamá handed her. "I'll be back in a little while with some breakfast for you. Call me if you need anything."

Mamá nodded. "I will. Thank you, Sarita," she said, closing her eyes again.

Softly closing the door behind her, Sara turned around and jumped slightly. "Devorah, you're up," she said, putting Mamá's empty cup next to the wash bucket by the door, and walking over to the fireplace.

Devorah nodded. "You shouldn't have let me sleep so long, Sara," she said, wiping off the table with a clean rag. "We have so much to do for Shabbat."

Sara waved her hands in the air. "You deserved some extra rest after that trip you took in my trunk," she said with a grin. "Besides, it won't take long to clean the house. I guess there is a good side to having so few belongings. We'll be finished in no time."

Devorah nodded, grabbing a battered basket from the corner by the door. "I'm going to get yesterday's wash off the line," she said, opening the door. "Then I'll finish up the mending, and start cleaning." With a wave, Devorah shut the door behind her.

Although Sara spoke bravely, she couldn't help missing the lovely things that always made Shabbat so special back in Cordoba. *Is some other girl going to eat in our dining room tonight with her family, and pick oranges from the tree in the garden?*

Sara gave her head a little shake. This was home now, and she was going to make the nicest Shabbat she could with the little they had!

"Now, what should I do first?" Her eyes suddenly fell upon Mamá's large wooden bowl that they used every week to make their Shabbat loaves. Pulling it out of a sack, Sara wiped it with a clean cloth, and set it on top of the table.

"Flatbread was easy with Señora Diaz's help on the ship. Will I really be able to make challah all by myself?" she whispered.

Sara looking longingly at the silver challah plate that stood on the shelf above the fireplace. "Remember, little plate, that after all the trouble I took to save you, I still have to bake the perfect challah to keep you as my own!"

Sara slowly mixed a little bit of yesterday's dough with some warm water. Then she measured the flour into another bowl, remembering to add some salt. She poured the water into the flour, working it with her hands until it formed dough. Then, as Mamá had shown her all those weeks ago in their kitchen back in Spain, she sprinkled some flour on top of the table.

"All right," Sara said aloud, looking down at the lumpy dough sitting in the bowl, "Here we go."

Lifting up the dough, Sara began to push it and pull it back and forth across the table's smooth surface. "Oh no," she groaned. The dough stubbornly clung to her fingers, just like it did the first time, back in Spain.

Sara stared unhappily at her hands for

a moment. "What would Mamá do?" she thought, knitting her brow in concentration. "I know," she cried aloud. Sprinkling more flour on her hands, Sara smiled as the pieces of dough on her fingers began to join the mound of dough on the table.

For ten whole minutes Sara pushed and pulled until the dough looked less lumpy. "This challah had better be perfect," she muttered between clenched teeth, as her arms and shoulders began to ache. Finally the dough was smooth and silky. "There, I did it," she declared. Sara put the dough back into the bowl to rest, covered it with a clean blanket, and wiped her floury hands. "I really did it!"

"Did what?" Devorah asked, opening the back door, and bringing in the basket full of clean clothes for Shabbat.

Grabbing one end of the basket, Sara helped her friend lower it to the floor.

"Devorah," she said, pausing dramatically, "For the first time in my entire life, I have kneaded the dough for challah, all by myself, and here it is!"

Sara lifted the blanket to give Devorah a peek at the dough.

Devorah smiled at her friend's enthusiasm. "Well, it looks good to me, but who knows how it will taste," she teased. "What if there's so much salt that we can't eat it? What if it's as hard as a rock? Do you think Señora Diaz will make some extra challah just in case?"

Laughing, Sara chased Devorah out the door and into the bright morning sunlight.

* * *

Later that morning, as Devorah and Sara were busy with the mending, Señora Diaz bustled in with packages from the market.

"Look, girls," she said excitedly. "Finally we can enjoy fresh fruits and vegetables again after the long sea voyage! And I brought you some fish for Shabbat."

"Thank you," Sara said. "I hope Mamá will have a better appetite now that we're no longer on the ship."

Señora Diaz went over to the big wooden bowl and peered under the blanket. "Why, Sara, don't tell me you're making challah by yourself!"

Sara bit her lip. "I wasn't sure if the dough was ready. What do you think?"

Señora Diaz pulled back the blanket and touched the dough lightly with her finger. "It's just perfect!"

She said the bracha, pulled off a small chunk of dough and threw it into the fire.

The two girls said, "Amen," and watched as the little piece burned black in the fireplace.

"I have some extra time today," said Señora Diaz. "Would you like me to finish this for you?"

"Oh, no," said Sara. "I mean, thank you, but I'd really like to try making it myself. You see, when I make the perfect challah, Mamá will give me her challah plate to keep. So you see, I really must try my best to do it without help."

The older woman looked at the silver plate on the shelf and back at Sara's determined face.

"Challah can be tricky, my dear. Just don't be too disappointed if your first try isn't quite perfect. Shabbat Shalom and good luck to you!"

After Señora Diaz left and Devorah went back to her work, Sara faced the bowl full of dough. It had grown quite a bit in the warmth of the kitchen. Sara poked it with one finger and it popped back up. "Exactly like Mamá's," she said happily.

Just as she was taught, Sara pinched off a little bit and put it aside for the next batch of bread. She divided the rest into three parts, and tried to shape the pieces into smooth, round loaves.

The first one looked more square than round. The second leaned a bit to one side, but Sara didn't give up. She took special care with the third loaf, handling the dough as she had seen her mother do it.

Looking up at the challah plate again, she took a deep breath. "Please, please, be perfect," she whispered. Sweat trickled down her brow as Sara struggled to keep her movements gentle and the stubborn dough nice and even.

"Well," she murmured, standing back and surveying her challah with a critical eye. "At least it's not falling to one side this time." Sara carefully put all the loaves on the blanket and wrapped them up.

She knew that peeking at the challah before it was ready would ruin it. So, although fairly dancing with impatience, Sara didn't go near the blanket for hours. She checked beans, cut vegetables, and helped Devorah. Finally, it was time.

When Sara unwrapped the blanket, the three little loaves were just as small and hard as when she'd shaped them. Her eyes filled with tears. She knew it was silly to expect her first batch of challah to be perfect, but couldn't it at least be edible?

"Oh, Sara," said Devorah, "I'm sorry." She knew how much her friend wanted the challah to be just right.

Suddenly, Sara had an idea. She carefully lifted the whole blanket and carried it closer to the fireplace. Would it work? Would those hard challah loaves grow the way they were supposed to?

The minutes went by so slowly, that Sara was sure time was standing still. She wouldn't allow herself even one little peek until she couldn't wait any longer. No one was around when Sara went over and gently lifted the blanket.

Her eyes grew wide with surprise... all three loaves had grown to almost double their size, just like Mamá's!

Proudly, Sara carried her challah outside to the oven they shared with so many other families. Some women she'd met on the ship were there, taking hot crusty loaves and soft white rolls back to their homes.

"Do you need any help, Sara?" one of the women called.

"Thank you, Señora," the girl answered. "But I'm trying to do this myself."

Sara put each challah onto the warm clay surface of the oven with a little prayer. "Please don't be as hard as a rock, and please taste as good as Mamá's," she whispered.

Sara stood by the oven the entire time, afraid her precious loaves would burn. Halfway through, she remembered about the water and rushed to coat the top of each challah and replace it in the oven to finish baking.

Poor Sara! Her face grew red, and her eyes smarted from the heat, but finally, the girl's patience was rewarded. Her challah was crusty brown and smelled wonderful as it came out of the oven. She carried the three loaves home, taking special care of the third one, the one that was perfectly round.

"Won't Mamá be surprised tonight?" Sara thought, as she hid the three loaves behind the blanket where she slept.

"Sarita," Mamá called suddenly.

"Yes, Mamá," Sara asked, wiping her hands hurriedly on a cloth, and opening the door to her mother's room. "Mamá, why are you out of bed?" she asked. Her mouth curved into a smile when she saw that her mother was dressed.

"How much time do we have before sunset?" Mamá asked, slowly walking into the kitchen, and sinking into a chair by the fireplace.

"A few more hours," Sara replied, pouring her mother a cup of water. "But Mamá, Papá said you need to rest today. Please don't get up yet. Devorah has cleaned the house, and the *arroz con garbanzos* is almost ready..."

Mamá looked at Sara's red face and straggly hair. "You're doing a wonderful job getting ready for Shabbat," she said. "But I want to do the mitzvah of helping to welcome the Shabbat Queen to our new home tonight. I won't do anything too difficult."

"All right," Sara said, a worried frown puckering her forehead.

"Señora Mizrahi," Devorah said, walking back into the kitchen, carrying a bucket of fresh water. "It's so good to see you up and dressed. Are you feeling better?"

Mamá smiled, as she began to spread a clean, white cloth on the table. "Yes, a little better, Baruch Hashem," she said.

Sara picked up the fresh fish that Señora Levine had dropped off earlier, and grimaced as the smell reached her nose. "I hope this *pescado* will taste as good as yours always does, Mamá," she said.

Mamá smiled. "I'm sure it will, Sarita."

* * *

Sitting under a tree later that afternoon, Sara closed her eyes and sighed. The comforting sounds of her neighbors preparing for Shabbat filled the air, and a cool breeze helped combat the heat of the late afternoon sun.

"Sara, there you are." Opening her eyes, Sara smiled as Yosef sat down next to her.

"Did you finish washing up for Shabbat?" she asked, wrapping an arm around Yosef's shoulders. "We have less than an hour before sunset."

Yosef nodded. "Why are you sitting out here?" he asked.

Sara shrugged, and leaned her head against the trunk of the tree. "I had a couple of minutes, and it's so cool under here," she said, closing her eyes again. "And I guess this tree reminded me of the trees that stood outside my window back home..." she said, her voice trailing off.

"Oh," Yosef looked up at the leaves blowing in the breeze. "Sara," he said a few minutes later.

"Mmmm," Sara replied.

"Are you ever... are you homesick too?" Yosef mumbled, trying not to cry.

Sara opened her eyes, and looked down at her little brother. "Yes, I am a little homesick, sometimes," she said, squeezing his shoulder comfortingly.

"Do you think this will ever feel like home?" Yosef asked, his voice cracking.

Sara smiled and pinched Yosef's cheek. "Absolutely," she declared, pulling them both to their feet. "This place will feel like home in no time, especially since I can still beat you to the door," she whooped over her shoulder, as she began to run across the small yard.

"Oh, no you can't," Yosef shouted happily, charging after his sister.

Giggling, Sara struggled to open the door, as Yosef tugged on her arm. "I win!" she cried, pushing her way inside.

"Sarita, there you are," Papá said, standing beside the set table, adjusting the worn but neatly pressed collar of his black Shabbat cloak. "Is everything ready for tonight?" he asked.

"Yes, Papá," Sara said.

Mamá walked slowly into the kitchen, looking rested, but pale. "How are you feeling?" Papá asked.

Mamá smiled. "Much better," she said. "Thanks to Sarita and Devorah, I didn't have to do a thing."

Sara smiled, as she placed the oil and wicks for the Shabbat flames in the middle of the small table. "Where is Devorah?" she asked.

"I'm right here," Devorah called, walking into the kitchen, her face shining clean from a recent scrubbing. "How much time is left?" she asked.

"A few more minutes," Papá replied, placing a small jug of wine on the table. "Yosef, come with me. We must go to join in the tefillot for Shabbat."

After they left, Mamá stood up slowly, and walked over to the table. "This is the first Shabbat we are spending in this wonderful land," she said. "May all our days be as peaceful and joyful as this one." The three of them lit the flames and recited the bracha.

"Shabbat Shalom," Mamá said. Her eyes were full of tears, but she was smiling.

Sara and Devorah hugged Mamá and each other.

"Shabbat Shalom," they answered.

* * *

"Moshe, what's wrong?" Mamá asked later that evening, as Papá sat back down before Kiddush.

"Well, I can't seem to find the challah," Papá said frowning slightly, as he peeked under the white cloth that covered the empty challah plate.

"My challah!" Sara cried, "I forgot to put it on the table!" She raced behind the blanket with the silver plate in her hand.

Everyone laughed. "I was a little worried there for a moment," Papá teased, merriment dancing in his eyes.

Biting her lip, Sara examined the

challah. "Everything looks all right," she mumbled under her breath, "but what if it tastes awful? What if it's too hard to chew?"

"Devorah!" Sara called, "Would you please put these on the plate and take them to the table for me?" she asked. "I'm too nervous."

"Sure," Devorah said, a puzzled look on her face. She placed the two beautiful loaves on the silver plate and carried them proudly to the table.

Sara's eyes were glued to her mother's face.

"Oh Sarita," Mamá breathed. "The challah looks perfect!"

"Really?" Sara asked, looking around at her beloved family. "But what if my challah doesn't taste as good as yours, Mamá?" Sara asked anxiously.

"I'm sure it will," Mamá said reassuringly.

"So am I," Papá declared, "Now let's make Kiddush and wash so we can all have a taste!"

After everyone washed, Papá picked up the challah and recited the *Ha'motzi*. Sara held her breath as Papá dipped a piece in salt and took a bite. "Perfect!" he declared. As was the custom, Papá tossed a piece of challah to everyone. It was a special way to show that food comes from Hashem.

Sara finally took a bite of her very first challah. As the moist, chewy bread filled her mouth, a wide grin spread across her face. "I did it!" she cried joyfully, throwing her arms around her mother. "I baked a perfect challah!"

"Yes you did," Mamá said, hugging her. "And now the plate is yours. May you always use it in good health."

"Oh thank you, Mamá," Sara squealed delightedly, picking up the plate and twirling around with excitement.

"Careful," Papá said with a laugh. "We don't want to drop that delicious challah." Sara gently lay the plate back down on the table, amazed that it was hers to use and to cherish.

"Oh Sara, how wonderful!" Devorah exclaimed, and Yosef smiled at his big sister.

Mamá and Papá looked at one another

across the table, pride shining in their eyes. "If Hashem decides to bless us with another daughter, may she be as wonderful as our Sarita," Mamá murmured.

"Amen," Papá said.

Sara looked at Mamá for a moment, her eyes widening in surprise. "Could it be?" she wondered, watching Papá and Mamá smile at each other. *Was Mamá expecting a new baby? That must be why she still needs to rest so much!* Sara felt this exciting secret bubble inside her, as she and Devorah served everyone the Shabbat meal.

As they ate and talked and sang, Sara felt she might burst with joy. Suddenly everything seemed so right... a new land, a new home, and soon, a new baby!

Sara gazed at the challah plate that had escaped the clutches of the evil Spanish Inquistion. Now it was hers, and someday, with Hashem's help, it would be her daughter's and granddaughter's and great-granddaughter's.

"Sarita, what is it?" Mamá asked. "You're not eating anything. Do you feel all right?"

"Yes, Mamá, I feel wonderful."

Sara smiled as she looked around the table at the beloved faces of her family. "We have each other, and we have Hashem's beautiful Torah and mitzvot," she said, "and that is more precious than gold."

Glossary

Aleichem Shalom – "Unto you, peace," traditional response to a greeting

Aleph-Bet – Hebrew alphabet

Av – Eleventh month of the Hebrew calendar

Baruch Hashem – Thank G-d

Batei Mikdash – Holy Temples

Birchat Hamazon – Grace after Meals

Bracha – Blessing

Challah – Sabbath bread

Erev Shabbat – Eve of the Sabbath, Friday

Gimmel – Third letter of the Hebrew alphabet

Ha'motzi – Traditional blessing before eating bread

Hashem – G-d

Hashem Echod – "...The L-rd is One," last two words of the Shema prayer

Havdallah – Ceremony at the conclusion of Shabbat

Kiddush – Sanctification of the wine recited on the Sabbath and holidays

Kohanim – Those who performed the service in the holy Temple

Mashiach – Messiah

Menorah – Candelabra kindled on the eight nights of Chanukah

Mezuzah – Parchment scroll inscribed with hand-written text of Shema, affixed to the doorposts of a Jewish home or building

Mitzvah/Mitzvot pl. – Good deed, one of the 613 commandments

Modeh Ani – Prayer of thanks recited upon awakening

Pesach – Passover

Shabbat – Sabbath

Shabbat Shalom – "Sabbath peace," a traditional Sabbath greeting

Shalom – Peace, traditional greeting

Shalom Aleichem – "Peace be unto you," traditional greeting

Shavua Tov – "A good week," phrase used at the conclusion of the Sabbath

Shema – The traditional "Hear O Israel" prayer

Shema Yisroel Hashem Elokeinu –"Hear O Israel, the L-rd our G-d..."

Tefillin – Phylacteries; leather boxes containing verses from the Torah, bound to the head and arm with leather straps during weekday morning prayers

Tefillot – Prayers

Tehillim – Psalms

Tisha B'Av – Ninth day of the month of Av, a Jewish day of mourning

Torah – Five Books of Moses; also refers to the entire body of Jewish wisdom, laws and teachings

Vav – Sixth letter of the Hebrew alphabet

Bibliography

Alvarez, Ana María López. Benito, Ricardo Izquierdo.
Plaza, Santiago Palomero.
A Guide to Jewish Toledo
Codex. Toledo, Spain. 1990

Gerber, Jane. **The Jews of Spain**
The Free Press.
NY, NY. 1992

Gilbert, Martin. **The Atlas of Jewish History**
William Morrow and Co.
NY, NY. 1992

Gitlitz, David M, Davidson, Linda Kay.
A Drizzle of Honey: The Lives and Recipes of Spain's Secret Jews
S. Martin's Press.
NY, NY. 1999

Goldstein, Joyce. **Sephardic Flavors**
Chronicle Books.
S. Fransisco, CA. 2000

Marks, Gil. **The World of Jewish Cooking**
Simon and Schuster.
NY, NY. 1996

Pike, Ruth. **Aristocrats and Traders**
Cornell University Press.
London, England. 1972

Searl, Janet Mendel. **Cooking in Spain**
Lookout Publications.
Malaga, Spain. 1987

Telushkin, Joseph Rabbi. **Jewish Literacy**
William Morrow and Company, Inc.
NY, NY. 1991

Twena, Pamela Grau. **The Sephardic Table**
Houghton Mifflin Company.
NY, NY. 1998

The publisher would like to thank the following people for their kind assistance with this project:

Elisheva Morrison, Historial Researcher
Yossi Eisen, Yasa Leah Fort, Yosef Fort, Ian Heiss, Rita Herman, Brad Perelman, Chana Perelman and Susan Polansky, Principal Lecturer of Spanish Language and Literature, Carnegie Mellon University.

OTHER EXCITING BOOKS
FROM
HACHAI PUBLISHING

Israel in the days of
King Chizkiyahu

Israel in the days of
the Maccabees

Spain • 1492

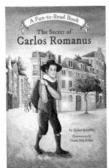

Amsterdam/Spain • 1650

Eastern Europe • 1800's

Russia • 1853

North Dakota • 1897

New York • 1905

WWI • Poland • 1914

WWII • Hungary • 1944

Canada • 1946

America • present day

Made in the USA
Middletown, DE
01 July 2021